# JORJA DUPONT OLIVA

# Chasing Butterflies

## IN THE MYSTICAL FOREST

Chasing Butterflies in the Mystical Forest by Jorja DuPont-Oliva
Copyright © 2014 by Jorja DuPont-Oliva
Copy Edit by Nancy Quatrano
Cover design by
Cover layout by Alexandra King
Interior layout and pagination by Michael Ray King
Chasing Butterflies in the Mystical Forest by Jorja DuPont-Oliva
220p. ill. cm.
ISBN 978-1-935795-33-9 (softcover) 978-1-935795-32-2 (hardcover)
Library of Congress Control Number: 2014951868



MRK Publishing
PO Box 353431
Palm Coast, FL 32135-3431
www.gowriteandyouwontgowrong.com

Printed in the United States of America

# Table of Contents

# **Table of Contents**

## Dedication


To my dearest friend
Rhonda Bracewell
Because you believed in me.

and also

To those who face their darkest hour…
Remember it's only a season.
It too shall pass

## Prologue

In the forest, creatures of the air and earth were gathered. The fall is turning the leaves of the forest hues of orange and golden brown, signaling to the creatures of air and earth that winter will soon be upon them. The first leaf to fall gently hovers as it descends to the ground. The creatures of air and earth prepare for what is to come by gathering nuts to store. Winter will soon cover the land like an icy blanket.

*"I am rooted to this earth as firmly as possible. I provide homes for creatures of air and earth. I provide sweet fruits, nuts, and rich saps to feast upon. I serve shade to soothe the flesh from the scorching sun. I enable lungs to breathe oxygen,"* **Tree Goddess announces to the creatures of air and earth who gathered at her base.**

* * * * * *

*"Wither and die my leaves must do. The thaw of the winter season will only strengthen my soul. My limbs and leaves will wilt and turn to compost, only to provide nutrients to my roots,"* **Tree Goddess explains to the creatures of air and earth as they scamper about to prepare for winter.**

Winter's cold harshness has devastated the land. All growth has died, creatures of air and earth are nowhere to be found. The anticipation of spring brings on the thaw, opening the land's heart to a stronger and healthier earth to pass on to generations to come.

*Winter shall pass and spring will gift me with succulent fruits, larger nuts, and richer sap. More room for the newly born creatures of air and earth to nest. Spring will also enable my wilted limbs to grow bigger and stronger to provide more shade and shielding and in return, oxygen as pure as the earth itself,* **Tree Goddess consoled herself.**

* * * * * *

Spring has arrived. The land celebrates. The creatures of air and earth join around the trees of the forest. They enjoy the coming of another year of unity.

*"As I die and wither each winter alone, it is only for a season. The more devastating the winter the greater strength I will have. The stronger I am, the more I can provide for our generations to come,"* **Tree Goddess says to the animals that now surrounded her.**

**The Butterfly, in a bouncy fluttering flight, gently lands on the tree's branch.** *"If only we could teach the humans to understand the lonely season and their hearts would not have to ache. They would know it is only a season and it too shall pass."*

Lonely she may be and that too shall pass...

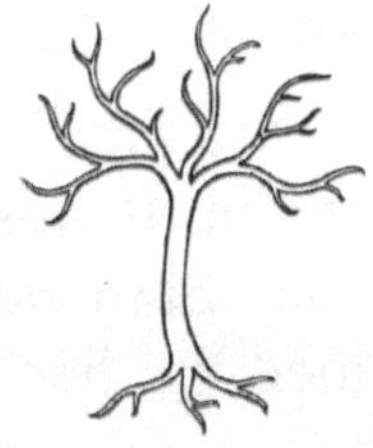

## CHAPTER ONE
### Lost

**Depart from evil and do good; seek peace, and pursue it.**
**PSALM 34:14**

*It's dark here. I'm stuck. I can't breathe. I can't move. Are those voices? Where am I? I hear music. OH... there's light, beautiful light...I can move. Yes... I'm floating. It is music, beautiful music...peaceful, loving, and forgiving. But, where am I...?*

Dee woke to butterflies and the smell of fragrant roses smiling at her from her bedroom window. The lone pine swayed from side to side, waving its needles like fingers to tickle her eyes.

She forced herself out of her bed and tiptoed to the kitchen, though she now lived alone. She did this out of the habit she'd formed during the three years she had roommates. They always slept later than her and both Lizzy and Ripley appreciated quiet mornings.

Lizzy, her best friend and business partner had been the last to leave. Dee conjured herself a cup of Lizzy's famous *fairy tale* tea, tea made out of herbs from her garden. Lizzy always said, "The tea is as magical as Dee's garden." A tea meant to regulate a woman's hormones, but Dee enjoyed the robust flavor. She didn't really believe her hormones had any problems.

Lizzy had married and just yesterday her husband Joe had moved the rest of her things out. It was almost like losing Lizzy with all of her things gone. Somehow, as long as some of Lizzy's things had remained in her room, Dee felt Lizzy's presence with her. Now, she just felt lost.

Dee still spent time with Lizzy at work almost every day but it wasn't the same. They were still good friends and loved each other dearly, but Lizzy went home to Joe and Dee went home to an empty house.

Dee took her tea into the garden and sat on the swing that she and Lizzy had built there. She hoped Lizzy would always be happy with Joe—but she knew first hand that being happy today didn't mean any long term happiness.

They had bought a house in the country which Dee thought a little odd. The funny thing was, Joe was a city boy, now determined to make himself into a *cowboy*. To Dee, it looked as though Lizzy's love of cowboys was giving Joe a run for his money.

Dee had been swimming in loneliness her whole life, except the years she'd spent with Lizzy and Ripley. Since she'd inherited her house, someone always lived with her or at least stayed on the couch-or something.

Leroy appeared in town about three times a year. Leroy drove trucks for a living. Dee spent time with him over the years but she knew he wasn't a keeper. She also knew it was nice to have him come around. Dee had lost her entire family by the time she graduated High School and since then, others she'd loved. She always suspected that her fate was to be alone. Every time she loved with all her heart that person would die-or get married. Dee gave her head a shake to quit feeling sorry for herself.

"I've got to get dressed. Lizzy wants me at BUCKETS early. Gotta get the tax stuff together for the accountant," Dee babbled aloud just to hear a human voice. She sipped the last of her tea, stood, and proceeded into the house to shower.

In short order, Dee was ready. She locked the house and jumped into her new truck. She'd bought her new red Ranger just last week. She took a whiff of that new car aroma.

She felt refreshed, having a new vehicle. She and Lizzy had driven around for years in Lizzy's daddy's old hunting Jeep. The new truck was a piece of the new path Dee traveled on...Alone.

It was back, the nagging sense that she was lost—not knowing what she wanted or who she was. Dee needed to figure out what she was missing.

After Ripley and Lizzy had moved out, she felt like a piece of herself had moved out with them and no matter how many pep talks she gave herself, no matter how busy she stayed, the feeling remained.

She pulled into the parking lot in front of their business and noticed the new sign being installed out front. It read, *BUCKETS* in capital letters and it was supposed to light up. The original sign could not be seen at night, so she and Lizzy decided to get one that would light up. They would light that sign up when they made the last payment to their private investor, Doctor Burger.

She felt a sense of pride for a moment. *Yep, BUCKETS is finally paid in full.* They were all earning a decent paycheck and so was BUCKETS.

"Looks good, fellas!" Dee hollered as she climbed out of the truck. She strolled to the front door and unlocked it with her key. She slipped through the door as though Lizzy might not notice she was late.

"Hey," Lizzy said with a smile when she looked up from the pile of papers she was attempting to organize.

"Hey," Dee replied. She pointed her thumb over her shoulder. "Sign looks good."

"I haven't gotten a look yet. It was still on the ground when I got here." Lizzy fumbled with the papers strewn all over the top of the green felt-covered pool table. She gave Dee another smile. "See if Gracey will work for you Saturday so you can come have dinner with us, okay?" she asked.

"Naw, I need the money."

*I say I'm lonely, then push people away.* Dee knew right then Lizzy noticed that something stirred around in her head.

"What's wrong?" Lizzy stopped flipping through papers and gave Dee a concerned look.

Dee sighed. "I am lost. I can't put my finger on it. I think I am in some kind of depression."

"It might be your hormones," Lizzy suggested.

Lizzy thought hormone imbalance was the reason for everything that wasn't right. "Can't be. I've been drinking your famous fairy tale tea, every morning," Dee replied with a slight chuckle.

"You just miss me," Lizzy said with a wink.

"As a matter of fact, I do. And Ripley, too. I realized this morning that I haven't lived by myself in a very long time.

"I'm lonely. Leroy only comes around when it is convenient for him." Dee started to nibble on her nails.

Lizzy stopped sorting the papers again. "Is that why you have been working more than you need too?"

"I guess," Dee answered and pushed herself away from the side of the pool table.

"Hey, let's go to the witch's town after we drop off the tax stuff. It will be like old times. What do you say?" Lizzy asked.

Dee knew Lizzy was *really* trying to comfort her. "Yeah, maybe that will make me feel better. Give me some direction." Dee grabbed the box of papers and waited while Lizzy turned off the lights.

Dee watched as her friend lock the door.

## CHAPTER TWO
### Vote of Confidence

*There is nothing either good or bad, but thinking makes it so.* **William Shakespeare, Hamlet**

"I just feel like my life is missing something. Like there's a big gap in my heart," Dee gasped as they pulled into the parking lot of the business center that housed the accountant's office.

"You will figure it out. I'm still here, Dee. I am *always* here for you. You know that," Lizzy said as she laid her hand on Dee's shoulder.

They stepped out of the truck, grabbed the years' worth of paper work, and treaded up the steps to the accountant's office. As they opened the door, they noticed a coffee shop next door.

"Hey, let's get a coffee when we finish," Lizzy suggested.

"Hope they have tea," Dee replied. "Hell... I'll get us a cup now, hold up."

Leaving Lizzy to stand in the hallway guarding their box of business receipts and forms, Dee darted through the coffee shop doors. She reappeared with two steaming hot cups in her hands and a donut hanging from her mouth.

"Now is better than later," she mumbled through the donut. She turned the knob and opened the office door that bore a tiger face on it.

As they strolled through the doors, pictures of tigers hung on all the walls of the office. "I see why she named her business THE EYE OF THE TIGER ACCOUNTING," Lizzy stated.

"I would say that is why," Dee said with a donut smile. Crumbles fell from her upper lip. Still sipping their hot beverages, they sat next to a table with a bonsai tree that separated them. A young girl came out and looked around as if the room was full of people. The young women waited.

"Are you the ten o'clock appointment...Buckets?" the girl asked realizing she had found them.

"Yes," Lizzy replied.

"You girls look awfully young to own a bar," The young girl stated, still looking unsure that she had the right people.

Dee waved her hand in the air. "We hear that all the time."

"How old are *you*?" Lizzy asked the assistant.

"Just turned twenty one," she answered.

"We weren't much older than that when we opened BUCKETS," Dee said with a nod and shoved the last of the donut in her mouth.

"Really?" the young girl asked with her head cocked as though she was now intrigued by the two of them. "That's *cool*. Maggie will be with you in a few minutes. She is on the phone. I guess it was pretty important."

Dee turned to Lizzy and smiled.

"Remember when we weren't sure what we were going to be when we grew up?" Dee whispered.

"I'm still not sure," Lizzy added and followed with a laugh. She sipped her steamy coffee.

Maggie finally emerged from her room of numbers and approached them with her hand extended.

"Hi, ladies. Ready to see how much money the government wants from you?" Maggie asked with a smile as she shook Lizzy's hand and then Dee's.

"I guess." Lizzy glanced over at Dee.

"Yeah, let's get it over with," Dee huffed.

They shuffled into the room and sat in huge, wheeled business chairs. After an hour of going through papers, Maggie peeked over the top of her accountant glasses.

"What in the world have you girls been selling?" Maggie asked. "Your sales doubled from last year's numbers. Usually business' drop down after the newness wears off, *but* BUCKETS is steadily increasing. Good job, ladies."

While Dee and Lizzy soaked up Maggie's praise, Maggie dove back into the papers. Eventually, she closed the folder, folded her hands on top of it and removed her glasses. A high-speed laser printer cranked out papers that seemed to go on forever.

"Everything looks good. Keep up the good work." She spun around and pulled the forms off the printer and placed them in front of the girls.

"Sign at the bottom where the arrows are and we are done." Maggie slid the papers across the glossy oak desk top.

Dee and Lizzy reviewed the numbers and signed where indicated. Dee pulled their checkbook from the box of papers.

"How much do we owe you?" Lizzy asked.

"Nothing for me, that is my gift to you, to celebrate BUCKETS being paid off. From EYE OF THE TIGER ACCOUNTING services. The red highlighted number needs to be paid to the IRS. I am so proud of you girls. I just want to give you this gift to help you in your adventures to come." Maggie said again.

"Thanks." Dee looked at Lizzy with surprise.

"Yes, thank you," Lizzy echoed. They stood and grabbed their box of papers, left Maggie's office and walked down the hallway towards the front door, still in a daze at Maggie's generosity.

The receptionist stopped them. "I'll try to come see BUCKETS when I get up that way." Her voice snapped them out of the trance.

"We'll treat you to your first drink of choice," Lizzy offered as they paraded out the door.

"That was awesome of her," Lizzy stated to Dee when they reached the truck.

"Yes, it was. Maybe I am too busy feeling alone to see the greatness of life. That definitely slapped me in the face." Dee smiled. "Let's go see what the witch's town has in store for us."

## CHAPTER THREE
### Trees

**Look up at the stars and not down at your feet. Be curious. Stephen Hawking**

They proceeded off the interstate, then turned down the long windy road into the witch's town where swaying ash trees welcomed them.

"Should we go to Madame Lefage again?" Lizzy asked.

Madame Lefage was the first medium Lizzy had ever experienced. The memory made Dee smile. Dee believed that was when Lizzy had become a believer in the world of the spirit realm.

Lizzy had been raised in a traditional Christian up-bringing, but she was still sorting out what she believed when she'd come to live with Dee.

Dee figured Lizzy was now a little more open minded, but still stuck to her traditional beliefs. Lizzy did a lot of reading about different religions and beliefs after the girls' first visit with Madame Lefage.

"I want to go right there." Dee pointed to an old hotel that had a little cafe in it.

"They do readings there?" Lizzy asked with a dumb-founded look.

"Yeah. I go on instinct, remember? That's where my gut is telling me to go."

"Then that's what we shall do." Lizzy smiled with a bobble of her head.

Dee felt like her old self again. *Why do I feel whole when Lizzy is around? Am I living off of memories? Or, is it this place, like time has never passed for us?*

She was analyzing way too much and gave her head a quick rattle. They got out of the truck and marched toward the stone steps of the old hotel. The gravel rocks crunched out a song of hope with each step.

The hotel French doors opened slowly, as though the doors had anticipated their arrival. The girls strolled through and stood in the lobby.

"Kind of creepy," Lizzy whispered.

Dee looked around. Old chairs with beautiful floral patterns lined the walls. An old musky scent mingled with the aroma of incense. A huge, faded and threat bare carpet sprawled across the hard wood floors. The place told a story of age; everything shrieked antique, even the chandelier that swooped down from the ceiling.

A little gift shop sat on one end of the lobby and a cafe on the other end, with a sign above the door that read, "Lost On Earth Cafe".

A little gnome-looking woman sat at an antique desk with glasses hanging onto the tip of her nose.

"May I help you ladies?" the women said glancing over the top of her glasses.

"Yes, we are here for a reading," Dee boasted with confidence, making her way to the counter. She'd learned young to follow her gut feeling and the hotel appeared to be the place she was supposed to be.

"There is Rev. Bonnie Eagle in room 228, available in ten minutes," the women said as her finger slid down the page of the log book.

"Oh, that's me," Lizzy blurted. "Instinct. Right?" Lizzy whispered to Dee.

The old woman continued. "Then, in about fifteen to twenty minutes we have Madame Ray available." She looked over the top of her glasses at Dee, as if waiting for an answer.

"Yes, that sounds good." Dee was distracted.

Dee heard strange mumbling moving around the room that distracted her for a minute. She would have thought it was people moving about, but the hotel showed no one there, but them and the gnome-woman.

Their appointments made, the girls settled into the old armchairs against the wall. Lizzy picked up a magazine. Dee closed her eyes to get her bearings.

From the grand stair case a woman dressed in a casual, yet elegant gown, floated down each step. Around her neck hung a necklace with an eagle charm that dangled.

"Do I have any appointments Elsie?" she asked the woman behind the counter in an accent Dee didn't recognize.

"Yes, the little blond over there," Dee heard Elsie say nodding in their direction.

"Lizzy, I think it is your turn," Dee whispered.

Lizzy looked up from the magazine. "Oh, ok. The eagle, which is why I chose her," Lizzy whispered back to Dee. She stood, then joined the Eagle woman. They disappeared up the stairs.

While Dee waited for her appointment, she browsed around the gift shop. Candles, stones, and books on every religion and spiritual belief filled the tiny shelves.

*Hmm, every religion known to man. Lizzy will have a field day here.* Dee enjoyed reading also. It made her feel less lonely. She picked up a couple of books.

As she strolled around the gift shop, she noticed some books written on religions of the world. There, peeking through many other books, stood a book on Native American Indian beliefs, which intrigued her, so she picked it up. The book had an American Indian peering at her from the cover. She opened it, began to read it.

The Native American Indian culture and beliefs seemed very similar to the way *she* believed. It made her wonder how she'd come to believe the way she did. *Was I taught?* Never the less, intrigued with the book, she took it to the front counter of the bookshop and bought it.

Before Dee could return to the lobby, the gnome-woman found her. "Madam is ready to see you now."

"Ok," Dee said as she grabbed the bag from the counter and walked out toward the woman at the stairs.

"Hello, I am Madame Ray. Have you ever had a reading before?" the women asked.

"Yes, many," Dee answered as they moved up the stair case.

Once inside, what appeared to be once a guest room, Dee sat in the chair across the table from another antique chair. She noticed pictures of trees geometrically placed on the walls. A lot of pictures of trees, in a grid pattern of some type. Mostly oak trees, though some were cedar and others were palms.

"You must like trees," Dee stated softly.

"Yes, I do. I believe trees represent an individual's life," the Madame explained as she made her way towards Dee.

"A tree has roots. Like our roots or ancestry; the trunk refers to our self, as a whole. The branches are the different paths we take throughout our lives." She gracefully sat across from Dee filling the empty antique chair. She reached for Dee's hands.

"Branches are relationships with people and paths we take. Trees bear fruit to feed on. They are very giving. They provide homes for insects and animals, as well as providing shade from the scorching sun." She held Dee's hands and closed her eyes. "The most important gift is they give us oxygen to breathe.

What type of tree do you feel you represent?" Madame Ray asked, her head cocked, wide eyed at Dee.

"Oak." Dee smiled. "I have always loved how they grow so large and look so beautiful, almost as though they have arms that want to hug you." Her smile broadened.

"I do see oaks in your life, one for certain. A very large oak... Its roots, so large they show from the ground." The Madame lifted her hands and hovered them over top of Dee's hands, as though she was covering them with a blanket of love.

"There will be a man coming into your life soon. When he comes, this tree's roots will be a significant part of your life." She waved her hands once more. "When it happens... you will know... It is going to change things."

Dee felt confused. *Could she be seeing Joe?* Things had changed for her when he came around. Maybe because she and Lizzy were so close. *Can she be reading Lizzy's vibes or energy or whatever it is they read?*

The Madam continued. "What do Butterflies mean to you? Wait, I see... Spirit tells me... Look at the stars. He will show you a butterfly," Madame Ray commanded.

Dee chuckled. "He is someone I loved very much. He passed." Dee took a breath. "Butterflies is our 'trade mark' you could say. So, I guess he is telling me I need to start looking up."

Dee knew that Madam Ray got *her* vibes and not Lizzy's. Then she continued. "You need to get more rocks. Spirit tells me you need more stones or rocks."

Dee laughed and said, "Yes another that I loved and lost. River Rocks was our 'trademark' as well."

"Play dolls... I see dolls and a little girl playing... spirit tells me to tell you to play." Madame Ray laughed as though something had amused her. "The oak tree is very important— spirit tells me there is a trunk or old chest, that if you find it... it will help you understand the tree better. Make the tree trunk whole again."

The medium looked into Dee's face. "I am not quite sure how."

Dee smelled a hint of roses.

"Ragged, Dee, Ann," the medium blurted out.

"Oh...I had an old chest that had Raggedy Ann stickers all over it as a girl," Dee said surprised, but confirming what the medium was seeing.

"Yes. Spirit says 'yes'. It is there you will find what you are looking for."

*What am I going to find there? Besides I have no idea where that old thing is anyway.* "Ok, I guess I'll have to go looking around for that old thing."

"Do you have any questions for spirit?" Madame Ray asked.

"I do. I feel lost. I am *so* lonely. I feel like there is something I am missing. Like I have forgotten who I am or like I forgot to put my underwear on." Dee twitched in her seat. "I can't put my finger on it, but that is how I *feel.* I need to find it or fix it. I need answers."

Madame Ray nodded her head as if she understood. "The trunk, no the chest, *is* your answer. You will find your closure. You are feeling this way because of the radical changes that your life has gone through the last few years. Wonderful changes you have gone through, and some that were terrible." Madame Ray took a breath and released it.

"Dear, I *feel* your struggle. The trunk..." Madam Ray shook her head as if to clear away her confusion. "I mean the chest is your answer." The medium closed her eyes and continued. "Like a tree, when branches die and break off they fall to the ground. They become compost for that tree. They dissolve into the ground and nutrients form to help the tree grow bigger and stronger. You are in that stage. Those branches are decomposing and so they will give your roots the nutrients they need. The trunk...I mean *chest* is going to help you grow new branches." The Madam bowed her head. She thanked God for her gift and Mother Earth for her deliverance.

Dee stood, still unsure of what she needed to do. *Except find that stupid chest!*

Dee was never good at tip toeing—that was Lizzy's job. Dee only knew how to jump into situations with both feet. Finding the old chest that she had as a girl, was going to be tedious. She had no clue where to start looking. This would definitely be one of those things that took time. Dee turned to exit the room.

Madam Ray stopped her. "Spirit also says that book will help."

Dee looked down at her bag with the Native American Indian book inside.

"OK... Thanks." Dee left the room still not knowing what direction she needed to take.

As she tromped down the staircase, she saw Lizzy in the gift shop looking at stones. Rose quartz to be exact. *Rose quartz is for love,* Dee thought. Dee made her way to Lizzy's side.

"How did your reading go?" Dee asked.

"Good, I guess. It's never what I expect, that's for sure. The Eagle lady told me to get some of these rose quartz, and to make pancakes. Can you believe that?" Lizzy said slightly irritated.

"Why? Are you and Joe having problems?"

"No. No problems. It's just that the newness has worn off. We know each other too well. We are fine. It's just not romantic any more. We are so busy working and taking care of the house and all the animals that we're too tired to enjoy each other's company. I'm sorry, I didn't want to vent to you," Lizzy ended in a worried babble.

Dee gave her friend a warm smile. She really wanted her to be happy for a long time. "You are at a plateau in your life, it'll come back. Sometimes you need to take time away from each other. Relationships need constant care. It takes work on both sides. Like Milly use to tell us, *marriage is a sixty-forty relationship. Sometimes you are the sixty and sometimes the forty.*

"I know. I have everything, yet, I still feel like something is missing," Lizzy said as she picked up a rose quartz to take to the counter.

Dee watched Lizzy pay for her purchase. *Lizzy just described my feelings to a T. We may be going down different paths but we're still struggling with the same feelings. Hmmm.*

"Lizzy, maybe it's the fact we are moving in different directions. We are somehow linked to each other besides through BUCKETS."

Lizzy turned to listen as Dee continued. "I mean, we did live together for six years. Maybe, because Joe hasn't taken you *dirt road dreaming* or *armadilla huntin'*. You *must* be having Dee withdrawals," she said with a smile.

"Yeah, we need to take a trip," Lizzy added in her devilish whisper.

"Then that's what we shall do!" Dee announced and they laughed, just like in the good old days.

## CHAPTER FOUR
### Thank you


*You may say I'm a dreamer, but I am not the only one. I hope someday you'll join us. And the world will live as one.* **John Lennon**


Over the next couple months they planned their trip. Summer was the slow season for BUCKETS, so it was as good of a time as any. With all of the responsibilities they had these days, planning things was a must. No getting in the jeep and taking off these days. Yep, they were growing up.

Gracey planned to tend to BUCKETS. They were only going to be gone a couple days. They decided to go to a bar expo in Orlando so they could use the trip as a business write-off. One day of their vacation would be business, the other one would be just for fun. The business aspect relieved their guilt and made it easier to get Joe to go along with it.

Dee procrastinated on looking for the Raggedy Ann chest. She thought deeply as she read her new book instead. The more Dee read the book she'd bought, the more questions she asked herself.

*How do I know so much about American Indian beliefs? Why do I feel so connected to this stuff? Is this where I find what I feel is missing? What could that old chest have in it to help me?* Dee was still unsure.

The only thing she was sure of, was that she was going on a vacation with Lizzy. That fact made her veins pump with life. *Just like the good old days.* This time they were going to take her *new* truck. *Maybe I should pull out my old beach umbrella for shits and giggles.*

Ripley had stopped by to bring Dee up to speed on her life. She and her daughter Lindsey were doing well. Lindsey's daddy, Walter, had moved out. Ripley didn't like the boringness of their platonic relationship.

About eight months after Lindsey was born, they became friends more than anything else. Ripley didn't seem upset about it, she said it was the best for everyone. Walter left, but he still wanted to be Lindsey's father, so he would get Lindsey part of the time. *I guess if it works for them...* Dee thought.

Yep, she sure missed her roommates. Ripley had moved in only a few months after Dee's mom had died. Back then, she was so numb from the pain everything was a blur. Maybe what I need to find is... Me again, she thought to herself. That's it.

As she searched for her suitcase she realized that she had put it in the attic after the last trip she and Lizzy had taken.

She lowered the attic steps and trudged up each step, not knowing what the hell she had shoved up there. *I'll look for that chest while I am up here.* Dee pulled the chain to turn on the light. It flickered a few times trying to build enough energy to glow. Dee glanced around for the suitcase and noticed it in the corner.

As she moved some things, she found a box that had Gina's name on it. Gina was Dee's younger sister—the one who had died in a car accident the year Dee turned thirteen. Gina, a girly-girl, had loved dolls. Dee slowly opened the box and felt a hint of her sister. There sat Gina's dolls. She always wanted Dee to play with her. A slight scent of Gina floated and tickled Dee's nose. At thirteen, dolls were baby toys to Dee. Dee took a seat next to the box. Gina's image appeared, smiling and sitting Indian style beside her.

"Gina, I'll play with you now," Dee murmured and cradled a doll in her arms. Tears gathered in her eyes. Dee slid a beautiful dress on the doll. She brushed the doll's hair.

Gina still smiled, sitting in her prettiest Sunday dress. The cutest freckles danced across her nose. After several long minutes, Gina slowly faded.

The sound of Gina's giggle taunted Dee's ears. The giggle floated across the room and landed on the left side of the attic. Dee turned her head to follow the sound and found where it had stopped. Dee spotted the Raggedy Ann chest, nestled in the far corner, exactly where Gina's giggle had landed.

"There it is! Cool. At least I know where it is," Dee mumbled to herself. She kissed the doll, stood, and grabbed the suitcase. She headed back down the steps, turned back and whispered, "Thank you, Gina."

Feeling just a little more peaceful than she had in days, Dee packed her suitcase and loaded it in the truck. She glanced across the street to the auto shop.

They were hanging a new sign over top of the mechanics shop. It read, *Johnny's Auto Repair*. Dee smiled and spotted Johnny up in the maple tree that stood next to the building. He had clipped some branches to make the sign visible.

"Do you like the sign, Ms. Dee?" he yelled from across the street.

"It's AWESOME, Johnny!" Dee yelled back.

Johnny had been doing well with that girl friend of his, Beth. She'd talked him into buying the mechanic's shop. Hell, he did most the work around there anyway.

"Have a great day, beautiful lady!" Johnny yelled.

"Thanks Johnny! I'm going to need an oil change after this trip with Lizzy. Should I make the appointment now?" Dee hollered back.

"Naw. Hell Dee, you get VIP privileges. Any time you're ready... I'll squeeze you in," Johnny replied.

Dee chuckled. *The Headless Horseman has found his head.* "I am damn proud of that fella," Dee mumbled. She strolled to her garden to give it a good watering before she and Lizzy headed out on their adventure.

The garden was still beautiful as ever. Butterflies fluttered as though they were having a party with the bees and the flowers. The roses were in full bloom. The passion flower thrived, their vines slowly creeping up the swing, as though it wanted to rock with Dee. She plopped down in the swing and said, "I love each and every one of you. I am blessed to have you here in my garden." She closed her eyes and enjoyed the peace of her magical garden.

She glanced across the street and pictured herself sitting on the hood of a car as Raymond worked on the body repairs.

*We were so in love...*

Today, Dee grinned because she'd gotten to love him before his time was over.

## CHAPTER FIVE
### *Peanuts in the Garden*

**Be faithful to that which exists within yourself. Andre' Gide**

Dee worked in the garden for an hour before Lizzy and Joe zoomed into the drive way in the candy-apple-red hot rod. Lizzy got out and skipped quickly to the garden.

"Wow it looks so beautiful. I miss this garden so much." Lizzy sniffed the air and twirled like a character from the Sound of Music.

"Wow Dee, you have a green thumb," Joe said as he followed behind Lizzy.

"Joe, I would love a garden at our house. I just don't know how to get it this beautiful," Lizzy said with one more twirl. Lizzy skipped to the swing and sat like a child on a playground.

Dee noticed Lizzy glance to the top of the pine to see if her eagle was perched there. Of course he wasn't.

"He has been coming around in the evenings," Dee said, almost knowing what Lizzy was thinking.

"Really? We have one on our property too. There is a nest. I thought it followed me out there," Lizzy whispered.

"It could have. They travel many miles in a day. Maybe that's why I am only seeing him in the evenings for a visit."

"Are you packed up?" Lizzy asked with a few kicks of her feet.

"Yep, just wanted to take care of the garden before we go." Dee gathered up her gardening tools.

"Looks like Johnny is doing good over there." Lizzy noticed.

"Hi Mrs. Lizzy, hey, Joe," Johnny called from across the street as he appeared out of the garage shadow. "Like the new sign?"

"Looks great!" Lizzy shouted back as she made her way to stand next to Joe.

"Good job, buddy!" Joe added as he waved to Johnny.

"Well Ms. Dee, you are going to take care of my lady, aren't you?" Joe asked as he grabbed Lizzy by the waist and hugged her from behind.

"Sure will, Sir." Dee saluted him.

"I am so excited" Lizzy giggled.

"You better miss me," Joe demanded as he spun Lizzy around and planted a kiss on her lips.

"You guys are nauseating," Dee groaned with a smirk on her face. She really enjoyed feeling the happiness they radiated.

"Look, a hummingbird," Lizzy pointed out.

"Yeah, there's a pair of them that keep coming around. I think there's a nest around here, somewhere," Dee added.

"I have never seen so many butterflies in one area before," Joe said in amazement.

Dee and Lizzy looked at each other and giggled. They shared that secret, no one else. It felt good.

"Magical, my dear Joe, magical," Lizzy said with one last twirl. "You see why I need a garden?"

"Okay ladies, you need to get on the road before it gets too late. Orlando traffic is hell during rush hour."

"Yes, you're right." Dee peeked at her watch.

"Then that is what we shall do," Lizzy exclaimed with a laugh.

"What have you done to this girl, Dee?" Joe asked squeezing Lizzy and kissing her like he couldn't let go. "She has been walking on clouds ever since she went off with you the other day, Dee."

"She was having *Dee* withdrawals," Dee answered with a wink. "She got her Dee fix, I guess." Dee thought for a second and realized she too, felt better. She and Lizzy had a bond. When they were around each other, their bond seemed to refuel them both.

Once they got on the interstate heading south, they chattered nonstop like teenagers.

"Thanks," Dee said as she glanced at Lizzy, then returned her attention to the road.

"Welcome." Lizzy laughed. "Remember when I first got to know you? You would *always* answer me that way. I never knew if you were being nice or mean. Of course later, after we became closer, I realized it's just you." Lizzy took a breath. "Thank you too." Lizzy looked over at Dee with a smile. "I wasn't sure Joe was going to let me run off with you. He acts like he is scared of losing me."

Dee's smile slowly faded as she realized that she understood where Joe was coming from. Then before Lizzy could notice what she was thinking, Dee said, "Hey you know that old guy that use to sell the boiled peanuts on the side of the road by my house?"

"Yeah he hasn't been there in a while. Gosh, it has been a *long* while since I've seen him there." Lizzy replied.

"His grandson came into BUCKETS on my Friday shift. He told me that the old man had a blood clot in his leg and the hospital sent him home and said it was nothing. The clot must have broken lose and went to his heart. It caused a massive heart attack and he died in his sleep," Dee explained.

"Wow, that's terrible," Lizzy whispered.

"He wasn't selling peanuts anymore because his grandson said that he complained his favorite customers stopped coming around. Two young girls in a Jeep that were full of life." Dee glanced at Lizzy.

"That is so sweet. Now I feel bad we couldn't do more," Lizzy said.

"No, it really was for the best. The grandson said he spent a lot of time with his grandpa the last couple years. He was glad those favorite customers moved on. Ironically, he did not know it was us," Dee remarked.

"Do you think the grandpa sent him to us?" Lizzy asked.

"Life has an odd way of making its circle, it seems," Dee replied. "Now, I have a peanut plant growing in the garden. So I would say, that he *did* send him in our direction. No peanuts yet, but I know they are coming." Dee glanced at Lizzy and smiled. Traffic got heavier so she studied the road, not Lizzy's face for a response.

Lizzy sat quiet for about a minute or two. "I read in a book—can't remember which book it was—but some beliefs say when you return, you come back as a plant or animal until it is time to be reborn as a human.

"Hmmm... Kind of odd." Lizzy sat looking out the window. Dee knew Lizzy was throwing questions at herself like she always did when something didn't agree with her Christian upbringing.

## CHAPTER SIX
### *Letting Go*

*We are all travelers in the wilderness of this world, and the best we can find in our travels is an honest friend.* Robert Louis Stevenson

"Wow, this place looks expensive," Dee gasped, her eyes wide and her mouth open.

"It does. When I booked us for the expo, they said this was the *cheapest* rate and the convention is right next door," Lizzy said, her expression amazed as well.

The glass exterior of the hotel seemed to climb and disappear into the sky. Around the base of the main tower marble fountains rested, each with a different aquatic creature spouting water.

They pulled into the driveway to the hotel parking lot, only after fighting traffic for the last hour. They both released a breath as though they'd just surfaced from a deep sea dive.

"Sure is a lot different from where we live, isn't it?" Dee said with a tired chuckle. She was excited, but a little frightened too.

"Oh, look! They have live pink flamingos walking around," Lizzy squeaked.

Dee added. "And a valet service. I don't see any place to park."

"Dee my dear, it looks like you are going to have to finally let someone else drive your new truck," Lizzy announced.

"I will park it myself." Dee grounded the words out through clenched teeth.

They pulled into the wrap-around drive that protected the entrance way to the hotel lobby. Dee locked her door and rolled down the window halfway to speak to the young man who made his way to the truck wearing a bucket shaped cap on his head.

"Where do I park?" Dee asked. Lizzy sat on the passenger side giggling.

"I will park it for you, Miss. It is against company policy to allow you to park it in the hotel garage. Sorry, I have to be the one to park it." He pleaded with Dee as he tried to open the door.

"I am a guest here," Dee pointed out, "and no one is driving my truck but me."

"Okay, Miss." He took a breath, surrendered and continued. "Across the street is where the over flow goes. You can park it over there." He pointed them in that direction.

"Thank you kindly," Dee said with a nod.

"Really, Dee?" Lizzy asked. "There were BMW's, limousine's and a lot of fancy cars. Do you realize how silly you just sounded? Nobody wants to steal a red Ford Ranger." She sighed and gazed out the window. "We'll have to lug the suitcases a mile, doing it this way."

Dee drove the truck across the street to the parking lot, pulled out their suitcases and locked it up. By the time they reached the lobby, she was out of breath and soaked in sweat. Maybe she was being just a little over the top?

"Ok...maybe tomorrow I'll get them to valet park the truck," Dee confessed as they entered the hotel lobby.

"Indulge, Dee! Pretend we're rich. They do this stuff all the time," Lizzy said.

But Dee was mesmerized by the size of the lobby and the expensive feel to it all.

"Wow this place is unbelievable." Dee exhaled starting to absorb it all.

Lizzy walked to the desk to check in. Dee wandered around admiring the fancy oil paintings that had to be at least twelve feet tall and four feet wide. A blue marble sculpture sat on a podium waiting to catch someone's eye.

Dee noticed Lizzy making her way back until a gentleman in a short black jacket intervened and took Lizzy's luggage. Lizzy waved Dee over.

*Okay, pretend I'm rich—they do this all the time.* Dee knew the man was going to take her stuff. *He works here and that's his job.* Dee continued to take deep breaths as she made her way toward Lizzy.

"He's going to take our luggage to our room, Dee. So we can go to a cocktail party. For the expo guests," Lizzy cautiously whispered.

"Ok...," Dee exhaled, though her chest continued to get tighter and tighter.

"It will be fine, I promise," Lizzy said softly as she pulled Dee's luggage from her tight grasp.

Dee smiled a smile that was as fake as Dolly Partons chest, but it probably looked good. "Did you say cocktail party?" Dee asked without breathing.

"Sure did, Ms. Dee." Lizzy soothed the moment.

"You always know what I need, Ms. Lizzy," Dee drawled and slung her arm around Lizzy's shoulder. They walked away from the luggage that was now in the hands of a stranger. She glanced back as if saying good bye to it.

Dee was having a hard time letting go of her things. For Dee it was *her* struggle. She felt that God had taken her family, Raymond and Brad. She had no say in that. Joe took Lizzy's heart and Dee knew that was out of her control, too, but her things? She *had* the say about that.

They walked through the lobby, down the long hall to a room called the Royal Banquet room. As they opened the double doors, the chatter of people floated into the hall.

People of all types stood about conversing about various wines and lagers. Dee felt like she'd entered the land of the giants and she and Lizzy did not belong there.

"We are the youngest ones here," Dee whispered.

"And *that* is something we should be proud of. Not scared of," Lizzy announced boldly.

"I know...I need a drink," Dee insisted and headed to the bar. Two young gentlemen were standing there, which helped Dee relax. They were young too, not quite as young as her and Lizzy, but closer to their age than the rest of the crowd.

"Hi ladies...are you here for the expo?" The dark haired man asked.

"Yes," Dee answered and turned to the bartender. "I'll have two Coors Lights, please." She turned back to the young man who had questioned her and replied. "We just arrived. This is my partner, Lizzy." Dee turned towards Lizzy. "And my name is Dee." She stuck her hand out.

"Lesbians," the blonde man coughed out under his breath.

"Nice to meet you, Dee and Lizzy," the dark haired one said with a nod. "This is Jared and I'm Aden."

Jared had sandy blonde hair and a mysterious grin or a scar that made his grin seem larger than it should be. Dee wasn't sure but it was familiar. Aden had dark hair and a dark complexion.

"Our boss paid for us to come," Aden said. "I'm a DJ at The Crazy Donkey and Jared is head bartender."

"Oh, I saw on the brochure that they are having competitions for DJ and Bartending at Pleasure Island," Dee announced.

"Yes, we are in it... The boss thought it would give us a little boost in experience to enter." Aden said. "What do you do?"

"We own a small pub north of here," Dee said with a sip of beer.

"Sure." Jared coughed through the mysterious grin again but this time more clearly.

"No really, we do," Lizzy said and Dee grabbed her arm not wanting to extend their conversation.

"Nice to meet you." Dee nodded and dragged Lizzy away from the two of them.

"They are jerks...Well at least that Jared guy is, anyway. I get a bad feeling in my gut, let's just stay away from them," Dee said.

"They are about the only ones even close to our age," Lizzy said looking intimidated with the room.

"Hey," Aden yelled and trotted over to Dee. "Sorry, Jared is an asshole sometimes. Maybe we can meet up later?"

"Yeah, maybe," Dee said over her shoulder as she and Lizzy walked away.

Dee tugged Lizzy to the other side of the room. "I don't know what it is, but that guy Jared spooks me," she said, glancing over her shoulder to make sure they weren't followed.

"Okay, okay!" Lizzy concurred.

"Sorry, that Aden guy is probably alright but that Jared...Oh my god, Lizzy..."

"What? What is it?" Lizzy asked as she grasped Dee's arm.

Dee wasn't much on showing fear but there it was. She could tell by Lizzy's expression that it was plain as day. Her heart pounded fast as a rattlesnake's rattle and dark memories closed in on her.

"Lizzy, remember me telling you about the things I dreamed when you saved me from dying? The visions...whatever it was I experienced? *That* guy was there... well not *him*...the grin. I remember that scar – that mysterious grin. I know it sounds crazy. Okay, I can't explain it." Dee sat her beer on a table and dropped into an oversized armchair. She gripped her head to think of a way to explain, but she didn't understand it herself.

"It's okay, Dee. I get it. We'll stay away from them. You always advised me to go with my instinct. So should you. I won't question your reasons. When you are ready to talk about it I'll listen...okay?" Lizzy placed her hand on Dee's shoulder. Then she lifted Dee's chin, looked her in the eye, and said, "Come on girl, we are on vacation! Let's have fun!"

Dee shook her head and forced a smile. "You're right. I just got a little spooked, I guess."

But much as Dee wanted to leave her darkness behind and have fun with Lizzy, she felt like a war was waging inside her. On top of her battle with loneliness, now she had the visions of her near death experience to deal with.

She was having a lot of dark dreams, unexplainable feelings of fear and a sense that something bad was about to happen. She ignored her instincts for fear that those dark dreams were going to come to pass, or was it that she was dealing with some kind of emotional imbalance?

She knew Lizzy would say it was her hormones, but Dee knew there was more to it than that. Talking to Lizzy about it was almost as frightening as handling it alone. She ordered another beer and began to relax a bit. She let Lizzy do the talking and tried to focus on the conversations around her.

They enjoyed the cocktail hour and listened to stories of the more experienced bar owners. Someday they'd be just like them.

"What's bothering you? Did I do something?" Lizzy asked.

"No. Gosh no. I'm not sure what's going on, Lizzy. I know I've been a bump on a log, but it's me. Maybe it's my hormones," Dee said with a smile.

She knew she wasn't ready to explain it all, at least not until she could figure it out for herself.

Dinner was a great treat. The hotel had a sushi bar down in the lobby and a nice coffee shop to boot.

"Wow Dee, this is just what we needed. A little reminder of the past to get us rolling again," Lizzy said as she threw her napkin onto her plate.

"I will have to say, I agree," Dee added as she flagged the waiter down for the check.

"And a business write-off too." Lizzy giggled. "I sure hope Joe is missing the shit out of me," she mumbled as she sipped her sake.

"Wow, Ms. Righteous...easy on the sake," Dee said with a smile. "It was a good evening. Thanks for not letting me fall into my black hole, Lizzy."

"You are welcome. Let's get the hell out of here. My pajamas are calling my name." Lizzy hiccupped. "The sake keeps adding curse words to my mouth."

"Then that's what we shall do," Dee added with a grin.

# CHAPTER SEVEN
## Angry Eyes

**Criticism may not be agreeable, but it is necessary. It fulfills the same function as pain in the human body. It calls attention to an unhealthy state of things. Winston Churchill**

*Oh no... I'm here again...is this sludge? Mud? Where am I? I can't move...She sees the mysterious grin in a black blob beneath her feet. No facial features, just that Cheshire cat grin and two glowing red eyes above it... Why? What does it mean? Beautiful music catches her attention. There is that beautiful music again...she looks upward... I'll be okay. Peacefulness floats over top of her body like clouds hiding the scorching summer sun for a second...*

Dee sat up in her bed, noticed the sun was starting to rise. She threw her legs to the edge of the oversized queen bed and paused to get a grip on the dream.

When she was a young girl her psychiatrist, Dr. Renee, would say, "Remember your dreams, they help you to figure out what is bothering you." So every morning like clockwork, Dee would sit on the side of the bed for a minute to reflect on what she had dreamed.

After her little sister Gina died in the car accident, Dee went to see Dr. Renee on a regular basis. Then, in her senior year when her mom passed, Dee started seeing her again to help her deal with the traumas in her life.

Dee really enjoyed her visits with Dr. Renee. They were more than therapy sessions—they had formed a friendship of sorts. Dee would still be seeing her if she hadn't retired and run off with that Nigerian fellow to some God-forsaken country in the Far East.

Dee stood and headed out of the room to a small kitchen and sitting room. When Lizzy checked them in, the hotel upgraded them to a suite. They both had their own room and shared a joining bath room that Dee was going to be the first to indulge in. Dee knew Lizzy was not much for mornings, so just like old times, she started the coffee pot and headed to the shower.

Hot steamy water ran down her face. She still visualized that stupid grin on that asshole's face. *Why am I letting him get to me? He was in my head while I was sleeping...now as I'm showering...good God, why?*

She violently scrubbed her face with water as if to wash her thoughts away, then let the water wash them all the way to the floor and swirl down the drain. That was a technique that Dr. Renee had taught her to clean away bad thoughts or feelings.

Dee was very angry in those days after Gina's death. She hated everyone and would think of terrible things she wanted to do. It wasn't to get attention like everyone would say it was. It was just what she wanted to do. Dr. Renee was the only one that understood.

She explained to Dee that it was negative energy and she needed to wash it away. Clean it off. A lot like dirt: if it stayed on her skin it could cause infections that could make her sick.

Dr. Renee was right. She said if Dee didn't wash it away she'd end up hurting someone, something or even herself. Dee knew what that dirt stuff was—it wasn't her—it was something trying to take her over.

As a little girl it was a scary feeling to think of that dark blob. *Oh my god... the dark blob with the eyes was in my dreams before I had my near death experience. I remember it well, now...*

After letting the shower pour over top of her to wash the thoughts away, Dee reached for a towel to wrap herself in, like a cocoon, she thought. She walked to her room to dress and noticed Lizzy sitting at the nook, sipping her fresh brewed coffee. She slowly shut the door, just enough to dress.

She yelled to Lizzy through the door. "What time is the seminar?"

"I think it's at 11:30. I'll check the pamphlet in a minute. I gotta get some coffee in me so I can see straight."

Dee appeared out of her room and sat at the nook with Lizzy.

"Had a dream again about that guy...the one with the stupid grin...Jared," Dee mentioned as she plopped down in the chair.

"Again? What do you mean *again?*" Lizzy asked with her coffee cup half way to her mouth.

"It's not *him* in the dream. It's that smile—evil grin or whatever it is." Dee sat up to explain better. "Over the years, especially at times in my life that I'm soul searching, or trying to balance myself. I dream of that smile... an evil grin...with glowing red eyes. That's why that Jared guy spooked me. Something about that grin he has."

Dee inhaled then released the breath slowly, hoping to maybe explain it a little better. "When you came and saved me the day I tried to kill myself...the nurses told me my heart had stopped beating and that they did CPR on me and when I came to, I was angry to be alive...I was, Lizzy—angry, hateful and I thought that the red eyes had finally gotten me." Dee looked out the hotel glass slider to see a beautiful palm tree swaying in the wind. She continued.

"Today while I was showering I remembered those eyes and the grin or whatever it is... After Gina had died... again after my mother's death...and again, yesterday."

"What do you think it means, Dee?" Lizzy asked.

"I don't know. What I do know is that it's not good or happy." Dee stared out the door and watched the trees. She needed to be outside with nature.

She stood and smiled at her best friend. "Hey, we have some time so let's go have breakfast by the pool."

Lizzy looked at her a long moment as though trying to figure out if she was going to be all right. Then she put down her coffee cup and got to her feet. "Okay, let me go get ready." Lizzy stood then turned back to face Dee. "Are you o...k... Dee?"

"Yep, I've got you, don't I? Besides I want God to smile on me for a little while," Dee said, feeling just a little bit better.

## CHAPTER EIGHT
### Changes

**I swear to you, there are Divine things more beautiful than words can tell. Walt Whitman**

The hot Florida morning sun and the smell of damp grass lingered around the poolside chairs. Dee sat back in the lounge chair with her shades on, while Lizzy sat up and watched children dive in and out of the pool.

"Joe and I are talking about having kids," Lizzy announced still watching the children play Marco Polo.

"Really? You two would have beautiful kids, Lizzy. Are you guys ready? I mean, for that responsibility and all..." Dee lowered her glasses to look Lizzy in the eye. Were kids something Lizzy really wanted or something she thought she was supposed to do? Dee knew Lizzy often did things that someone else wanted her to do and not necessarily what *she* actually wanted.

"Well, Joe mentioned it. I want kids for sure, always have. I just don't know if I'm mature enough to be a good mother," Lizzy said finally responding to Dee. "I guess I'm a little scared is all. I know I can do it. I know I'll be the best mom I can be."

"So do it then." Dee relaxed to her sunning state.

"I'm scared it will take me away from Buckets, you, and even Joe... Kids are a lot of work. Example, look over there at that woman. She looks exhausted and as soon as she sits back down to rest, one of the kids yells for her to take care of something for them." Lizzy finally reclined in the chair.

Dee lifted her glasses to watch the woman and then lowered them. "Yes, she sure does look tired. I feel bad, almost guilty that I am enjoying myself today. Lizzy... Just enjoy now and stop worrying about tomorrow. I am sure that women has more love for those kids than any tiredness could faze."

"Yeah, you're right. If we decide to do it, then I'll worry." Lizzy exhaled.

"That breakfast sandwich was awesome, with the egg and ham. What was that sauce it had on it again?" Dee asked.

"Hollandaise sauce. That was an Eggs Benedict sandwich. I believe it's an American dish. It was originally known as a cure for hangovers in the mid to late 1800's. By some Wall Street guy named Benedict. My grandmother used to tell us that story when we were kids." Lizzy giggled. "The things I remember her telling me. She must have known I was going to need to explain it to you, I guess."

Lizzy's grandma had been full of stories. She always had a good tale to tell. That was how they got the idea for BUCKETS. That beautiful story of her friendship with the young, women tavern owners. Dee grinned thinking about the story Lizzy's grandma had told them years ago. *Now we are that story.*

"It's about that time, Lizzy," Dee glanced at her watch.

"I need to do a quick change," Lizzy announced as she grabbed her towel and slid on her flip flops.

"Not me, I'm going just as I am." Dee peeked over the top of her shades and smiled.

"Okay. I'll meet you back here in about ten minutes."

As Lizzy rushed away, Dee drifted off. She thought of the years back when she and Lizzy would go dirt road dreaming.

And all of the heart to heart talks they had. Then something dawned on her.

*If Lizzy had never had her heart broken by Lee, and Raymond hadn't died...would we have become this close of friends? Buckets would never have been. Oh gosh—I would actually have killed myself.*

"Hi," a voice interrupted.

Dee opened her eyes. Through the tint of her sun glasses she saw Aden standing in the same spot that Lizzy was minutes before.

"Hello. I hope you didn't bring that friend of yours," Dee blurted out as she ripped her shades from her face to look around.

"Sorry to say, he isn't far behind me. That's why I wanted to come say hello before he ruins it for me again." Aden chuckled. "You guys going to the seminar at 11:30?" he asked as he took a seat in the lounge chair next to Dee.

"Yeah. Lizzy went up to change. As soon as she gets back we're heading in that direction." Dee sat up and noticed Jared coming towards the two of them. *Be nice Dee, Don't let him see that his asshole-ness is getting to you.*

"Cool! I'll see you over there then. Real quick, what are your plans for tonight?" Aden asked with a quick glance over his shoulder.

"Not sure yet," Dee answered. "Here's your friend now," she announced with a nod.

Aden stood. "Nice to see you again. Maybe we could hook up later?"

"Yeah, maybe," Dee answered.

"What'sup?" Jared said as he approached the two of them.

"Hi," Dee stated with a smile as tight as a zip lock bag. *Be nice, be nice.* With her lips still sealed she nodded at both young men.

She stood. "See ya over there." Then she slipped her feet into her sandals, folded her towel and placed it in her bag. She looked up and saw Lizzy making her way to her.

*Thank God... Lizzy always saves the day.*

## CHAPTER NINE
### Secrets

**What is a friend? A single soul dwelling in two bodies.
Aristotle**

The seminar was at least an hour long. Dee wasn't all that impressed with the ideas and promotional stuff they had talked about. *Maybe if these people would actually work their business they would know what needed to be done to make the customer happy!* She glanced over at Lizzy who was taking notes. *That girl...still trying to do things the right way.* Dee chuckled to herself and looked away so Lizzy wouldn't notice, but she did.

"What?" Lizzy whispered.

"Just think, being here is not teaching us a thing," Dee whispered back. "These people own chains of bars. Own them and that's it. They don't have a clue how to run one." She popped a life saver in her mouth. "We've learned more in six years than all of these old timers even know."

"Yeah, but it's giving me a different perspective," Lizzy said quietly, putting her palm out for a lifesaver.

Dee handed one to Lizzy, then looked to the front of the conference room and saw Aden on the other side looking at her.

She smiled and sat up from her slouching position. She nodded her head as a hello to that side of the room.

*How long has he been watching me? Gosh I hope I didn't do anything embarrassing.* Dee straightened her shirt that had crumpled due to her position in her chair. *Now I sound like Lizzy.*

"They do have a *few* good ideas," Dee whispered out of the side of her mouth.

Time ticked by and finally it was over. They could now go check out the expo hall. It was a gigantic room filled with all the new bar promotions. From mechanical bulls and glow in the dark wine glasses, to every new craft beer on the market. Yep, they could have samples. And sample they did.

Lizzy found an area that had coin operated photo booths just like the ones she remembered as a young girl. She told Dee the booths had been on the boardwalk in Daytona Beach.

Every spring break she would go and come back with pictures of herself and her friends squeezed in that tiny booth, so tight, they weren't sure if everyone was able to fit.

Dee noticed the new booths were slightly different though. These photo booths would morph two people's pictures and make it into one person. Sure enough, Lizzy made Dee do it. As they were waiting for the picture to develop and pop out the side, Lizzy pulled out a picture of Joe. She stuck two dollars and his picture into the slots on the booth next to the one that she and Dee waited for.

"What the hell. I'll get a glimpse of what my kids will look like." Lizzy glanced at Dee as she straightened the money for the machine.

"It's ready," Dee announced as she watched the Dee-Lizzy picture slowly present itself. Dee stared at it. Mesmerized by it.

Together, they *were* the perfect female figure. Lizzy's beautiful blond ringlets with Dee's cinnamon red hair made the most beautiful color. Lizzy's rounded eyes morphed with Dee's green eyes show a gentleness. Together they looked like an angel sent from heaven. A soft gentle glow surrounded the perfect female figure. Lizzy walked over to see what Dee was so dumbfounded about.

"Wow, we are beautiful together!" Lizzy said to Dee as she took a look at the picture.

"I know...we *are* beautiful together. Perfect female," Dee whispered with a tear rolling down her face. She was so glad, at that moment, that Lizzy had saved her from killing herself years before.

Suddenly, the next morphed picture popped out. Lizzy took it out and stared. No expression on her face, she just stared. Dee made her way to Lizzy to see what had her so frozen. Dee glanced at the image.

"Wow! That looks just like your nephew when he was little. When we first met," Dee said trying to break Lizzy from the spell she was under.

"It does..." was all Lizzy could say as she stared at the photo.

"These photo booths are pretty cool," Dee said still pacing around trying to break the spell. She knew Lizzy was imagining having a child. Lizzy was always trying to figure out her future before she actually needed too. "Come on, let's go check out the frozen drink machines they have."

"Yeah, yeah...ok," Lizzy mumbled finally tucking the picture in her purse.

As they passed by exhibit after exhibit of great new products, they stopped to consider what to take back to BUCKETS. *Now this is what I think is the best part of all of the expo conference crap*. This is where the new idea's and promotions happen, Dee thought.

Of course, Lizzy had to stop at all of the kitchen displays. They had a hot air fryer that cooked the food in under two minutes. Dee knew Lizzy was eyeballing one of those to take back. Of course, money wasn't an issue, but lugging it back home would be. Lizzy grabbed a bunch of paperwork instead to consider getting it at a later time.

They proceeded on and found an area which had a special gum display which interested the girls since the legal limit for alcohol consumption had just been lowered. If someone was considered drunk on two beers, business was really going to suffer. The gum was designed to prevent your alcohol content from showing up on a Breathalyzer.

They walked over to check out the miracle gum. Of course, they had already sampled quite a few beers and wines so Dee knew she was at an illegal alcohol limit. Sure enough, it worked. They chewed the gum, then blew in the Breathalyzer. Neither one came up over the legal limit.

"There has to be a catch," Dee said.

"Look, it still hasn't gone through FDA approval yet," Lizzy read.

"Yeah they won't let that secret get out," Dee added as they proceeded to the craft beer section.

"Look, Magic Beer!" Dee laughed. It was a beer with a dark rich nutty flavor and included a fortune at the bottom of the bottle.

Lizzy finished her last sip and read, "Your life will bring you back to your childhood."

"Now that's funny!" Dee laughed and took her last sip. "May the secrets of life, answer your question," Dee read and then wrinkled her nose. "Come on..." She started moving toward the frozen drink machines still thinking about her fortune. *Secrets, my whole life has secrets.*

"Lizzy I was thinking...I may try to find my father," Dee blurted. She stopped and Lizzy took two steps to catch up.

"My mother never gave me a lot of information as to why, when and how. I just think maybe that would fill this gaping hole that I seem to have inside me."

Lizzy just listened in silence. *Is she scared to tell me what she thinks?* "Well? What do you think?" Dee asked.

Lizzy was straight faced and looked as though she was looking at a ghost. "Dee, if you feel you need to, than that is what you should do. I'm not good at this stuff, you know, giving advice." Lizzy inhaled a breath.

"I will say this, I don't want you to get hurt. It frightens me. He may not be wanting to find you. I don't know if that would be healthy for *you*." She exhaled.

"I know...." Dee started walking again. She knew how much Lizzy wanted her to be happy, but she also knew how much Lizzy wanted to protect her, if she could. "I am preparing myself for that."

Silence floated between the two of them like an invisible butterfly. Dee spoke again. "All I can remember is my mom standing on our porch, holding me, talking to a man that stood on the lawn. His face is fuzzy in my mind, but I know he was good. I was only a baby but I felt love for him...somehow I know that. It sounds crazy but instinctually, I don't think the stories my mother told me about him were true."

"Then you need to do it," Lizzy said. They walked in comfortable silence until Dee spoke again.

"Oh yeah... I forgot to tell you, or just didn't want to think about it...Leroy... he's married."

"What?" Lizzy yelled.

"Shhhh...." Dee put her figure to her lips. "I hadn't heard from him in a while, so I called..." Dee hesitated then continued. "A women answered, said he wasn't available. So I said I was doing a survey and asked her if she could talk to me. I asked questions—he has two kids, Lizzy."

She looked away, ashamed to tell everything she had learned about sometime-lover, Leroy. "Seems he has been married for a long time...I am so ashamed. I really didn't want to tell you."

"Dee, *we* had no clue...it isn't your fault," Lizzy added.

"Hell, at least he isn't dead, that's the good news. You know me and my track record – fall in love and boom, they're gone for good." Her laugh was a half-sob. "I did care for him, though," she whispered.

Finally they reached the frozen drink machine section of the exposition hall.

"Well girl, we can't drown our sorrows, but let's see what these fizzy things taste like, what do you say?" Lizzy said with a sad smile.

Dee could tell Lizzy was hurt and betrayed by Leroy's deception, too. They had shared each other's pain in the past. That's what made them perfect females when they were together.

## CHAPTER TEN
### Pleasure Island

**The final proof of greatness lies in being able to endure criticism without resentment. Elbert Hubbard**

Hours later, and many frozen drinks later, the young women staggered back to the hotel to freshen up before the bus ride to Pleasure Island.

Pleasure Island was owned by Disney as sort of an adult entertainment park. It was an island of bars—every type imaginable. A disco bar, an 80's bar, and even a country western bar. Each and every night would be like a New Year's celebration.

The expo sponsored an event that offered contests for all of the expo attendees. They had bartending contests and DJ mix-offs. They had dance competitions and karaoke sing-offs. To Dee, that was definitely the best part of the expo besides the fact they had VIP badges that entitled them to drink free all night.

"We can get some dinner when we get over to Pleasure Island. They have *got* to have food there," Lizzy babbled as they were making their way to the shuttle bus.

"Thank God we don't have to drive. I might have even had to settle for the valet parking tonight," Dee chuckled with a slight slur. "I have to admit I'm a little tipsy."

"A little? You put your shirt on backwards. Twice!" Lizzy giggled over her shoulder at Dee who trailed behind. "Thank God I caught it before we headed out of the hotel room," she teased with a chuckle.

They climbed aboard the shuttle bus and searched for seats together. Two empty ones sat in the far back, so they made their way along the aisle, giggling with each step. Lizzy seemed a little less intoxicated than Dee, but Dee had more reason to indulge in the frozen drinks. She had a world of darkness she was struggling with.

As they took a seat, Dee glanced across the aisle and there they were, Aden and Jared, smiling at them with a look that said they knew the girls were drunk. Dee gave them her zip lock smile again knowing alcohol tended to make her speak her mind. *Be nice, be nice.*

"Hi guys!" Lizzy chirped.

"We were just wondering if you guys were coming tonight to watch us compete," Aden said.

"Yeah," Jared interrupted. "I'm definitely gonna win that bartending contest. It's in the bag for me. I'm the best in south Florida. At least that's what I'm told," he finished with his evil grin.

*What an asshole! He wishes he was the best! Arrogant ass.* Dee sat with her mouth sealed. She smiled and nodded because she was afraid what might spew out if she started to speak.

"Cool, we'll have to check it out. There are a few contests we wanted to watch. It really depends what's happening when you compete," Lizzy added.

*Good cover Lizz...*Dee nodded. "Yeah, a lot of the contests are going on at the same time. We'll just have to wait and see."

She sealed her lips again as she looked straight ahead. *Careful Dee, silence is best.*

"They are such bitches, Aden. Why you wasting your time?" Jared whispered loud enough for Dee to hear.

*Ignore him.*

After a few minutes, the shuttle bus slowly pulled into the entrance of Pleasure Island. The shuttle door opened to a fantasy land of bars. The smell of roasted peanuts, hot popped corn and sweet cotton candy floated in the air. An adult play land, Dee thought.

As they walked through the entrance way, Dee noticed Lizzy's amazement at the size of the buildings and the outside stage that was setup for concerts. Dee wondered if Lizzy was visualizing Joe on the stage.

"Pretty awesome, huh?" Dee asked.

"Yeah, very cool!" Lizzy said. "Let's check out the country western bar first."

Dee chuckled. "Wrangler man, right?"

"I know I'm still into the wrangler man look. Did I tell you I got Joe a cowboy hat for his birthday?" Lizzy giggled.

"No...Did he like it?"

"Well, he never said he *didn't*. He just stared at it. Then he thanked me. You know Dee, maybe I did go a little overboard with the wrangler man thing. I just knew that was a safe relationship. Maybe, I know I'm safe with Joe too. I never claimed to be normal, I just tried to act the part, as much as possible," Lizzy stated.

"You weren't *normal*, you were righteous and rigid, member?" Dee laughed. "Come on, it'll be like old times. Can you remember any of those line dances Johnny taught us?"

"Maybe," Lizzy said with a grin.

They headed to the country western bar first. As they sauntered through the swinging wooden saloon-type doors, the smell of saw dust lingered about. There were stools shaped like saddles. A live country band squeezed comfortably onto a small center stage. Large belt buckles winked a sparkling shine on almost every patron in the place. Ten gallon hats on some, and maybe, five gallon hats on others. As they glanced around for a place to sit, a tall cowboy shuffled over to them.

"Would one of you ladies care to dance with a cowboy? Two steppin' is my specialty," he drawled. He put out his hand for one of them to take a hold of.

"No, thank you, I'm married," Lizzy said firmly.

"It's only a dance, little darlin'," he replied, taking his hat off and placing it over his heart.

"No, really, we just wanted to have a drink and relax some," Dee said. She grabbed Lizzy's hand and pulled her along to the bar. She knew Lizzy felt uncomfortable about the guy not taking no for an answer.

"Thanks, Dee," Lizzy whispered.

"Welcome," Dee whispered back. She signaled for the bartender to bring two beers.

## CHAPTER ELEVEN
### Words


***Associate yourself with people of good quality, for it is better to be alone than in bad company.* Booker T. Washington**


They made their way across the street to the eighties bar that promoted the DJ competitions. Unfortunately, with the beers they'd downed at the country and western bar, the alcohol guided their way. The fact that the DJ competition was happening totally slipped their mind.

As they walked in, they heard a lot of old high school favorites. Lizzy grabbed Dee's arm and dragged her to the dance floor. In the eighties, everyone danced and no partner was needed. It was a Cindy Lauper song, "Girls Just Wanna Have Fun."

"God Dee, I so wish I would have enjoyed my high school days and not been so stuck up Lee's ass," Lizzy yelled over the music as she danced.

Nothing like a song-and intoxication-to make you feel like a teenager again, Dee thought. "Me too...I mean... Lizzy, I really never lived... until I died." She gave Lizzy a smile, but Lizzy had stopped dancing to listen.

"I mean, I had a hard time enjoying my youth. I hated high school. I hated everyone, including myself." She grabbed Lizzy's hand to get her dancing again. "Come on, I am just being honest. This music brings back bad memories and feelings for me."

"Well, let's go then," Lizzy announced. She tried to pull Dee's hand to get her off the dance floor.

"No! I'm making new memories now." Dee smiled. "Let's dance, girlfriend." She knew Lizzy had a hard time dealing with Dee's darkness - or any darkness for that matter.

She decided she would quit dwelling on her sorrow for Lizzy's sake. She knew that sometimes it helped her when she could talk it out, but maybe tonight wasn't a good night to do that.

*They were having fun.*

The DJ announced the kick off to the evening's DJ competition. Dee and Lizzy made their way off the dance floor and straight to the bar where two stools welcomed them.

"I'll have two beers, please!" Dee ordered. She swung around to face the dance floor and there stood Aden, face to face with her.

"Hey, you made it," he said. Lizzy swirled her stool around when she heard his voice.

"Um, yeah," Dee babbled, then turned to sip her beer.

"Hi, we didn't realize... Yeah, just in time, I'd say," Lizzy corrected herself.

"So where are they doing the bartending competition?" Dee asked to make sure she and Lizzy knew not to show up at that one. Aden was a good guy, but Jared was a pure bummer.

"At the Baja Club across from the disco bar, nine thirty." Aden said as Jared reached around behind him and covered his eyes.

He made some remark in Aden's ear, then he smiled that evil grin at the two of them.

Dee bet he was drunk. *Not only an ass, but now a drunk ass.* She was careful not to let her face show her disgust.

"Wha'sup?" Jake asked with a nod.

Both girls gave him a tight-lipped smile and continued to talk with Aden. Then he was called to the stage for the competition. Jared casually moved away and the girls were thankful of that fact.

"Aden seems to be a great guy, Dee."

"Yeh...he's nice. He seems to make good money. Did you know he was just telling me, he works for a big distributor during the day and DJ's at night? He owns two houses, and has a 401k that he plans to retire on," Dee added. "He definitely has his shit together."

"He seems interested," Lizzy sang.

"I think you and I both know, he is too good for me, Lizzy."

"What is that supposed to mean?" Lizzy asked.

Dee could tell she was a little pissed. At least her drunk voice sounded that way.

"Doesn't matter. There's someone I've had a little interest in. He comes in at happy hour, almost every time I'm working," Dee said to get off of the subject of Aden.

"Does he have a tattoo, long hair and rides a motorcycle?" Lizzy asked with a roll of her eyes.

"Yes...that's him!"

"Really, Dee? All the guys you're attracted to look like that," Lizzy added as she sipped her beer.

*She is right. Why do I like the bad boys?* In the back ground was Aden's voice DJ-ing the next song.

"Wow, he is pretty good," Lizzy said.

"I was thinking the same thing." Dee smiled. "Maybe he wouldn't be half bad to date. He only lives a couple hours from us. Maybe I do need to date someone that has their shit together rather than what I'm attracted too."

"You are too hard on yourself, Dee. Lighten up... *you* taught *me* that," Lizzy said.

"You knew what you wanted in a man. That list you had was longer than a road to Hawaii," Dee said.

"There's no way a road can go to Hawaii," Lizzy argued.

"And there is no way a man like that exists!" Dee said with a hearty laugh. "I, on the other hand, don't have a clue what I want...*Or* I'm scared if I find another one, I might lose him. Not like I don't have that sort of track record. " Silence suddenly separated the two of them. *Again Dee, Pushing your darkness on Lizzy.* She broke the silence.

"I like the bad boys, the rebels, and the Bonnie and Clyde things, because I know what I'm getting. They can't disappoint me, or hurt me. They don't expect any more than what I am capable of giving. Mainly I'm scared to love like I did with Raymond and Brad," Dee said peeling her label off her beer. "It's not fair to them." Her voice crackled. Raymond and Brad were two of Dee's first loves and they passed away at very young ages.

"I understand, Dee. I just don't agree. You're a beautiful person and deserve beautiful things, which is all I am saying. Do you hear me?" Lizzy said spinning her stool to face Dee. "Please, for me, start thinking a little more positive. I feel like you are drowning yourself with negativity. Find that Dee that I know and love. She's still there."

Lizzy lifted Dee's chin with her fingertips. "You are the controller of your feelings... Sometimes sadness can suck you up and you will never escape it. That is why I always write. I write it out, then burn it or throw it away. Kinda like getting rid of the sadness."

Dee could feel her eyes filling with tears. Even if it was the alcohol, she wasn't a crier. Thankfully Lizzy stopped talking and sipped her beer.

Dee did the same.

## CHAPTER TWELVE
### Grip of Fear


***We are made wise not by the recollection of our past, but by the responsibility for our future.*** **George Bernard Shaw**


The disco bar was just around the corner. Dee and Lizzy headed out onto the cobble stone street. They noticed a woman in a booth doing hair wraps and braiding hair into corn rows with beads.

"Come on, let's get our hair done." Lizzy bounced in front of Dee as though she was being maneuvered by a hyper-active puppeteer.

Dee laughed and shook her head. "I don't know…it looks painful. The corn rows, that is. I don't know how those colored folks do it all the time to themselves."

Lizzy had gotten a few steps ahead of Dee and spun around to walk beside her. "Well, maybe...I just want to do a hair wrap. Curls are hell to braid."

Dee shrugged. Maybe a change was exactly what she needed. "Yeah, what the hell, I'll get corn rows. It'll be something they can talk about when we get back home." She laughed as she warmed to the idea. "The regulars at BUCKETS will think we lost our minds, Lizzy."

They approached the woman. Dee went first because corn rows took longer to do. Dee was glad she'd had so much to drink because sure enough, it was painful. Her scalp felt like it was being pulled so tight her head was going to pop off. She picked out tiny blue beads with specks of gold to put on the ends of the braids.

"Hey guys!" a voice called from the sidewalk that bordered the cobble stone street. It was Aden without Jared.

Dee looked up from having her chin tucked into her chest while the woman added the beads.

Lizzy turned to look, then took the words right out of Dee's mouth. "No Jared?"

"Nah, he had to go early to get the bar set up for the competition," Aden said. "Looks good, Dee...makes your eyes stand out."

"Thanks." Dee stood to pay the woman and Lizzy sat down to get her hair wrap.

"You guys coming to watch Jake?" he asked as he lured Dee a little further away from Lizzy.

"Umm, I don't think so. You did great in your competition," Dee said to change the subject.

"Yes, I got second place," Aden said as if figuring they'd left before the winners were announced.

"I know, we left right after you were announced," Dee explained. "Jared came over and started with his obnoxious self. We had to dodge." Dee tried to just be as frank as possible. "Look... you are an awesome guy, but we can't stand Jared. So I'm sorry to keep disappearing on you."

"I get it. I don't like him much either. I guess you could say I'm stuck with him for the next...two more days," Aden said with his hands in his pockets. He poked the toe of his shoe at roots that had grown through the cobble stone road.

"I'm done!" squeaked Lizzy from behind them.

Dee turned, surprised. "That's all you had done? Your idea, and that's it?" Dee asked, feeling her temper rise. Her hair was so corn rowed and beaded that her eyes were going to pop from her skull and Lizzy's idea of a radical change was a *single* hair wrap?

"Yep, a hair wrap," Lizzy squealed again pulling on the single wrap that was attached to her hair. What made it worse was the fact she was twirling it and smiling like a little girl. She had no idea how annoyed Dee was.

*If I didn't love her so much, I would choke the life out of her right now!* Dee turned her Jared-smile on Lizzy and stuffed her hands in her front pockets. *Breathe, Dee, breathe.*

The three of them crossed the street and entered the disco bar.

"Gotta love the disco balls! We need to get one for BUCKETS!" Dee yelled over the music to Lizzy, who still twirled her hair wrap around her index finger.

"I love disco...as a young girl Lynn and I had paper feet to teach us disco steps. Hell, we never learned, but sure was fun," Lizzy yelled back.

"Never cared for it," Aden said. "My parents were hippies, so when disco was *in* I was listening to free love songs." He laughed as they walked over to the bar.

After many drinks and lots of laughter, the night came to a close. The three of them headed to the shuttle bus. Aden grabbed Dee by the arm to allow Lizzy to get a few steps ahead, then turned her to face him and planted a kiss right on her lips.

Dee didn't fight the kiss and even enjoyed it. She liked him a lot, but she also knew he was way too good for her. Besides, she couldn't bear the idea of falling in love again, only to know he'd die just when life was beginning.

"What's up guys?"

There stood Jared. His eyes glowed as red as fire with that evil grin.

"Hey," Aden said, turning toward the voice. "I was about to head over and meet you. I just wanted to talk to Dee real quick."

Dee heard an almost guilty, scared tone to Aden's voice. Then she realized that Aden had spent the entire evening with her and Lizzy. He'd missed Jared's bartending competition.

Dee decided it was a good time to leave. "Hey guys, I'll see you back on the shuttle. Lizzy's probably wondering what happened to me." She turned and headed towards the shuttle before they could answer.

She caught up to Lizzy who had never realized that Dee and Aden hadn't kept up with her. She was still babbling about disco. Alcohol tended to put Lizzy in her own little babbling world, but it always made Dee smile.

Once they were on the shuttle and seated, Dee watched as Aden and Jared boarded. Aden smiled a quick smile, then sat in his seat. Jared followed staring down at Dee with the glaring red eyes of a wolf ready to pounce.

She quickly looked away. *He is bad...real bad.* Her stomach knotted and fire moved quickly up to the center of her chest. Her heart pounded so hard she could hear it in her ears. Overwhelming fear flooded through her body, so intense she started to panic. *Hard to breath. They're back.*

The panic attacks were back. She'd lived the majority of her life with the attacks but it had been years since her last one.

*Oh my god—Not since the day I tried to kill myself.* Her panic increased.

"Are you okay, Dee? You're shaking." Lizzy voice sliced through the panic.

"I just need to get back to the room, as soon as possible," Dee groaned through clenched teeth. "I have a horrible feeling, like something bad, *real bad* is about to happen," she whispered.

"Of course, straight to the room," Lizzy slurred.

Dee knew Lizzy didn't understand, but there was no way she could explain right then. *I will be okay...I will be okay...* she whispered over and over.

## CHAPTER THIRTEEN
### Instincts

**Thinking will not overcome fear but action will. W. Clement Stone**

The shuttle arrived at the grand hotel. After everyone ahead of them had exited the shuttle, Dee stood and let Lizzy step in front of her, to block her fear.

It was very late, but the lobby still seemed to have people buzzing about. Dee noticed a holly tree in a planter outside the lobby entrance that looked as if it was slowly dying from neglect. Much like she felt about herself.

"Straight to the room, Lizzy." Dee hated hearing her voice trembling in fear.

"Okay, okay," mumbled Lizzy.

They walked to the elevator, waited for it to open. Dee glanced all around them to see where Jared had gone, but was nowhere. The doors slowly opened and they entered quickly, then pressed the floor number. The elevator doors shut and Dee sighed with relief. *What the hell is wrong with me?*

"Are you sure you are okay?" Lizzy yawned.

"I will be as soon as we're in our room with the door locked." Dee exhaled evenly.

*He's following us. I know it. I feel it. He's watching me. Why am I so paranoid? What's happening to me?* The elevator doors slowly opened.

There he stood. Jared, red eyes, evil grin and all.

"Hello ladies!" he announced in a drunken voice.

Alarm bells sounded in Dee's mind and she grabbed Lizzy by the arm and pushed her way through to keep from being cornered.

"What's the hurry?" he asked, picking at his teeth with a tooth pick.

"I thought you guys' room was on the ninth floor," Lizzy slurred.

"Let's. Just. Go. Lizzy." Dee gripped Lizzy's arm and pulled. They left Jared behind and hurried off to their room.

Dee glanced back a few times to see if he was following but he just stood near the elevator and watched them. At the last glance, he was gone.

When they got to the room Dee locked the door behind them and exhaled a sigh of relief. Of course, Dee knew Lizzy didn't understand her fear, but that was fine. They were safe.

Lizzy staggered her way to her room and flopped down on to her bed and fell fast asleep. Dee could now rest her mind in peace. She closed Lizzy's door and went to her room.

She went to her room, undressed, and said a prayer of thanks as she snuggled herself safely into her bed.

## CHAPTER FOURTEEN
### The Light

**Fear is that little dark room where negatives are developed. Michael Pritchard**

*He's coming for me. I know, he's close. It's so dark. How will I ever be able to see him if it is dark? God help me see...*

Dee awoke suddenly and sat up, realizing she was dreaming last night's fear all over again. She took a moment to convince herself it was a dream.

She looked at the clock and noticed that she had slept in. She *never* slept in. Of course, between the alcohol, the dancing and the fear, she'd been exhausted. She listened to the quiet. Had Lizzy slept in, too?

She crept out to the kitchen nook and no Lizzy. She turned to the door. It had been unlocked. She tiptoed to Lizzy's room but Lizzy was gone. Her panic attack returned and she struggled to swallow around the lump in her throat. *I will be okay...*

She busied herself making coffee and even then, with it still hot in the pot, there was no Lizzy. Dee walked to the window and looked out to the valet parking area.

At least ten police cars hugged the front of the building. *Oh my god, no, please no...* Red and blue flashing lights flashed like the disco ball she'd adored last night. She began to tremble with panic.

The hotel room door opened and Lizzy quickly shut it behind her. Fear and dread masked her face.

"Oh my God, Dee...something horrible happened last night. *Here*. Here, right here..."

Dee watched Lizzy's hand clutching what smelled like breakfast sandwiches. The brown paper bag shook so hard Dee thought it would fly across the room.

"What is it? What happened?" Dee asked as she moved to grab the food before Lizzy dropped it. Dee helped her to a chair before she crumbled.

"There was a rape. The girl was beaten. So bad, she almost died. If the valet guys hadn't found her she probably would have. I saw her...they were loading her in the ambulance. Oh my God, Dee. It was awful!" Lizzy said rocking back and forth with her arms wrapped tightly around her waist.

Then she stopped rocking. "They think they got the guy. Someone saw a guy enter the lobby last night with blood on his fist."

"Look at me Lizzy! Calm down. I have double-locked the door. We're fine. We're safe. We will pack our things and go home as soon as this mess clears away. Okay?" Dee squatted down in front of her to get her to focus.

Dee was always the one to handle things in a calm way. Except last night. *I knew my instincts were on to something. I knew it.*

Dee paced to the window several times to see if the police had apprehended anyone. Finally, Dee spotted them escorting someone to a police car. It *was* Jared—Dee would recognize that hair color anywhere. Dee watched as Jared looked up to her window, right where she stood. His red eyes slowly dimmed.

The officer placed him in the back seat of the police car and closed the door.

"Oh my God, it was that Jared guy!" Lizzy exclaimed over Dee's shoulder.

Dee just nodded silently.

"That could have been us, Dee!" Lizzy hissed.

"I know. I know," Dee said. "But, it wasn't. It was *not* us! So let's just be thankful. Let's have a cup of coffee, calm down and then we'll go home. Okay?"

Lizzy looked at Dee, fear still evident in her tear-filled eyes. "We can't tell Joe about this. He'll *never* let me go away again."

Dee watched Lizzy babble her way to her room.

## CHAPTER FIFTEEN
### Evil Plant

**They are like trees planted by streams of water, which yield their fruit in its season... In all that they do, they prosper. Psalm 1:3**

Dee and Lizzy returned home from their mini vacation, summer ended and fall graced them.

They stepped back into their day to day responsibilities with no mention to Joe what had happened at the hotel or the fact they had met the man who had done such a horrible thing. It was their secret.

Dee woke early Wednesday morning, made a hot cup of herb tea and sat down to go over her itinerary for the day. Although BUCKETS wouldn't open for at least three more hours, she had tasks that needed tending.

First off, the garden needed her love and care. After the garden work, laundry needed to be washed, folded, and put away. And, last but not least, she'd need a quick shower before she headed off to BUCKETS. *Oh and I need to put the empty suitcase back up in the attic. I'm tired of tripping over it.*

"Okay Dee, get to work," she said aloud as she stood from the small kitchen table. She swigged down the last sip of tea and marched to her room to dress in her gardening cloths.

Out the screen door she went. She headed to the garden and noticed a strange plant growing. It wasn't near most of the other flowers and plants, but it was there.

Unlike any of her others, it was spiny and crooked and almost had a ridged look. She knelt down to take a closer look.

A sudden flash of the darkness—the muck—she fell to her knees. Now even closer to the plant there was a flash of red glowing eyes—the ones she had seen so many times in her nightmares.

Dee jumped back so fast she landed on her butt. She inhaled the sweetness of her garden, but only for a moment. *That plant is not good. It's bad. It's downright evil.*

That very moment she stood and grabbed a shovel as tears rolled down her face. Panic took control and she dug with short, angry, chopping strokes to rid it from her garden. Breathless and overwhelmed with fear, she stopped shoveling and proceeded to pull every last root from the dirt as quickly as she could.

She bundled them up. With her arms full she dashed to the fire pit at the back of the house and tossed everything in there.

"You are not going to take over my garden!" she declared to the plant. She wiped the dirt from her hands and pulled a pack of matches from her pocket. She needed to burn the evil plant. She lit the match and threw it into the pit. She could almost hear the plant screech for mercy.

Still shaking, Dee watched from a few feet away. She overturned a clay flowerpot and pulled out a pack of cigarettes, shook one out and lit it. Her secret vice for sure, but she really needed this one. She finished her smoke and tossed the butt in the pit.

"Done!" She walked away as the squalling and screeching continued. She finished weeding and watering her garden and returned to the house. The slam of the screen door behind her reminded her to put the suitcase back in the attic.

She tugged on the rope to the attic door and unfolded the steps, then lugged the suitcase up the steps and searched for the dangling light chain. When she pulled the chain, the attic lit up. Looking around she noticed how she had neglected so many items that was stored up there. Old photo albums were full of memories that might trigger emotion. All the items stored up there were things she had tried to forget about, but now demanded to be noticed again.

*Maybe now is the time to grab the chest.* That was a big step for her. It was scary, but needed to be done. There it sat in the corner where her baby sister Gina's giggle still lingered. *What can it hurt? I'll grab it now. Doesn't mean I have to go through it now. I'll just grab it for now.*

That was exactly what she did. She stared at it the whole way down the steps. *I'll take it one step at a time. What if I don't like what I find? One step at a time, Dee.*

When Dee talked to herself she always did it in third person only because she heard voices and that was how they spoke to her. She always knew which one was *her* true voice because it sound just the same as her own.

When spirit talked it wasn't a voice as much as it was a sound or rhythm. In her darker moments, it was more of an angry pounding sound. It seemed to her that the older she got, the more she was learning to listen and understand better.

"Gosh it's getting late...I need to get showered up and get BUCKETS opened," Dee said out loud to the glowing clock on the stove. She set the chest on the table and off she went to get ready for work.

Before leaving, she took one last trip to the back of the house to make sure that the evil plant was now ashes. It was nothing but red kindling ash and she did a quick spray with the hose that hung attached to the back of the house.

Dee breathed easier. Even the fire pit and fire hose were Lizzy's idea. Lizzy always worried. *Just in case the fires get out of control,* Lizzy would say.

*Thank you, Lizzy.* Girl, you knew I'd need this one day, Dee thought to herself. The sizzling and cracking continued as Dee walked away and hopped in her truck.

## CHAPTER SIXTEEN
### Small Steps

*Never doubt that a small group of thoughtful, committed citizens can change the world. Indeed, it is the only thing that ever has.* **Margaret Mead**

The chest set on the kitchen table for a week or so. The more Dee starred at it the more it seemed to call out her name. She just ignored it. It was time for work Dee dressed and headed for the door and glanced once more at the chest. After a quick stop at the bank Dee headed to BUCKETS. She pulled the truck into a parking place and glanced up at the new sign. She thought back to the first day she and Lizzy had opened BUCKETS.

The girls had found an old antique store on the side of the road. Brad and Jessie had cut them such a deal on the buckets, the girls bought everything they had. The young men had even helped them get set up. They were friends. And more. Her dear Brad and Jessie.

Dee heard Jessie had married and moved to West Virginia to build a log cabin close to the stream.

The stream where Brad had told her that he loved her. *I love you, Dee,* she still felt Brad's voice say. She sat in the parked truck for a moment.

Many times she heard the voices of the ones she had loved and lost. *Is that them trying to come through?* She shrugged. She would accept that for what it was. "I love you too, Brad." She slowly exited the truck, walked to the door of BUCKETS and looked around.

She noticed how fast their town was growing. Cars buzzed through their town more so now than ever. There was even talk of adding another traffic light. National news even had a segment of the fastest growing towns in the nation and their town was one of those mentioned.

Dee unlocked the door, flipped on the open sign and strolled further in. The smell of stale smoke and the noise of the music from the night before still lingered. From the look of the bar stools, it looked as though people had just left. *Lizzy must have been busy last night.*

She retrieved the change from her back pack and headed to the register. After setting up the register with small bills, she did a quick inventory of the beers. The beer distributor always showed by lunch time to get the order, so she was going to be prepared.

Lizzy was due in at any time with the soup of the day and hopefully some fresh produce from the market. On the shelf behind the bar was the picture of Brad and his buckets calling to her to hold them. Dust had covered it and Dee wanted to see his face again, so she wiped the dust from the picture.

"Yep, eye candy," Dee said aloud and smiled as she replaced it on the shelf.

"Hey, I didn't get a chance to clean good last night. We were busy up until I closed," Lizzy exhaled as she walked in with handfuls of groceries from the market. "Once I get the soup started, I'll get it looking good for ya."

"No biggie, I already wiped down the bar," Dee added as she followed her to the kitchen. "Been thinking a lot about my family's past and I finally brought down that chest to go through it."

"What did you find?" Lizzy asked. "Anything about your father?" Lizzy stopped to get an answer from Dee.

"No, I mean, I got it down from the attic, I haven't opened it yet. Been starring at it for a week or so."

"Why not?"

"Lizzy, I need to take this slow. What if what I find, isn't what I *want* to find?" Dee asked before turning away to leave the kitchen.

"Dee, you need to do what feels right for you. Instinct remember? You taught me that." Lizzy smiled. "When you are ready you will open it. Until then, you are one step closer. It's out of the attic right?"

"Yep, I guess I *am* one step closer." She stood in a moment of silence. "Maybe I'll unlock the hinge tonight." She laughed.

"Yeah, small steps. You got this girl," Lizzy added. "Now go...I need to get the soup on for your lunch crowd," Lizzy said with the swish of her hand.

Dee walked out of the kitchen and straightened the bar stools. The door opened and in walked Ripley.

"Hi. How was the trip?" she asked.

"Good, it was fun. Mostly, anyway. We three need to get together and go to dinner or something. We miss hanging out with you." Dee smiled. "How is Lindsey doing in school? Is she adjusting to the fact her daddy isn't staying with you guys anymore?"

"Yeah, I guess. She seems okay with it. He comes and gets her quite a bit. And school is great, she is a whiz. Already reading...in kindergarten," Ripley added. "Oh here." She handed Dee two envelopes. "They are invitations to her birthday party. She said it wasn't a party without you, Lizzy and Joe. I was just going to invite her friends from school, but she insisted that I invite my friends too." Ripley chuckled. About that time Lizzy poked her head from the kitchen door.

"Hi Ripley! How's Lindsey?" Lizzy asked wiping her hands on a paper towel.

"She's good. She wants you guys to come to her birthday party. I gave Dee the invitations. I have to get back to work—we have a delivery coming soon and Jacob doesn't know the difference between a can of paint and a hammer." Ripley kissed her hand and blew it to Dee then to Lizzy as she walked back out the door.

"Bye!" Lizzy yelled.

"We love you!" Dee called and turned to Lizzy. "I hate growing up, we end up getting sucked up by responsibility and have no time to enjoy each other's company anymore."

"I know, that's what worries me about having kids. Joe has mentioned it again," Lizzy announced. "I'll admit I'm considering it."

The front door opened again before Dee could reply. Two older gentlemen walked in. They didn't look familiar. *Must be new to town.* These days there were a lot of new faces. The town was growing and so was the population. Dee made her way to them and offered them the BUCKET special. Seems they were looking around the area to open a chain sports bar. A lot like the one the next town over had. Big fancy sports bars. With TV's everywhere and kitchens that had 10 cooks. Yep, it sounded as if BUCKETS was going to have competition in the near future. This scared Dee a little but she wasn't going to worry until it was time to worry.

Moments later a battered-looking women walked in with some handmade jewelry she wanted to sell. The "gentlemen" ignored her as if she was a peasant. Dee made her way over to her to see what she had. Dee looked at the bracelets and saw the women had spent many hours attaching the beads to each one. She bought one for herself and one for Lizzy. The woman turned to leave and said, "May God bless you," and then shuffled through the door.

One of the gentlemen sitting at the bar said, "You bought that from her? She's just going to go spend that money on drugs or alcohol."

"And what if she spends it on milk for her child? I can't be the judge of how she spends it. I can pay her for the time she took to make it," Dee remarked as she admired the beautiful bracelet.

Dee and Lizzy always believed that Doctor Burger gave them the chance to own BUCKETS, so why not pay it forward?

Lizzy made her way out of the kitchen with the smell of fresh hot chicken noodle aromas following behind her.

"Smells yummy. Is it ready?" Dee asked

"Yep, want me to scoop you up a bowl? I made extra with cooler weather coming."

"Nah. I'll get it, besides you work tonight. Go home and rest up before you have to come back." Dee made her way to the kitchen.

"Hey I wanted to tell you some good news." Lizzy followed behind Dee. "My sister met this really great guy. He loves the kids. He owns his own business too."

"That's great. It's about time she found someone, and the fact he is good with the kids is even better," Dee said as she scooped up her bowl of soup, then grabbed a spoon. The soup steam vaporized into the air. Dee blew on the spoon to cool the soup just enough to sip the broth.

"He makes really good money at his business. He has a phone in his car too," Lizzy said. "I was thinking that maybe we should think about getting one of those car phones. If we aren't here and Gracey needs us, we would be only a phone call away." She smiled at Dee.

"Even if one afternoon we wanted to go dirt road dreaming. Who knows what else we could come up with if we had the chance to dream again?" Lizzy twitched her eye brows like

Groucho Marx. Dirt road dreaming was how the idea of BUCKETS had come to light for Dee and Lizzy, and Ripley was the one to come up with the name. In those days they were young women looking for their place in the world.

"Are they expensive?" Dee asked.

"I'm not sure, but I could find out for us. Are you interested?" Lizzy asked.

"I'm interested in finding out if they are expensive, first." Dee snickered, then blew on her spoon again.

Lizzy glanced out to the bar to check if everything was okay, then turned back to Dee. "Wow this *new* you is really doing a lot of tip-toeing these days. First the chest, now the idea of a car phone." Lizzy giggled. "Back in the day you just jumped in with both feet. Remember the shirts you bought before we opened? Our names, the color, even the style – you never even thought to ask me or check on anything at all, you just did it."

"I know, my instincts have been fogged. Crazy how I can't tell if my hunches are mine or coming from some dark side." Dee's smile vanished. *I can't believe I just said that!* She blew on the spoon again and smiled as if it was nothing. *I hate that I can't explain this to her.*

Lizzy looked at her closely and seemed satisfied that Dee was all right. She reached for her purse.

"Okay. Just think about it. I think it would benefit us, besides we need to catch up with the times," Lizzy said as she fished her keys from her purse.

"Yeah, let me think about it," Dee said as she set her bowl down and made her way down the bar to check on the guys that were seated at the end.

"You guys want another round?" she asked them as she smiled and waved Lizzy out the door.

## CHAPTER SEVENTEEN
### All Grown Up

**The cave you fear to enter holds the treasure you seek.**
**Joseph Campbell**

Hours later Lizzy returned freshly showered and ready to work.

"Hey! Were you busy today?" Lizzy asked as she hooked her purse strap on the coat hook in the kitchen.

"Not busy, but sold a lot of buckets. Seems everyone is in a down mood today. Even old Henry drank more than his one beer a day," Dee smirked. "Lizzy, I'm kind of nervous about opening that chest when I get home."

"You have been stewing over that all day haven't you?" Lizzy asked, putting her hands on her hip and looking very authoritative.

"You are going to be a great mom, Lizzy." Dee laughed out loud as she tried to explain. "I swear I just saw your mother in you." She clutched her stomach because she was laughing so hard.

"Very funny, smarty pants." Lizzy pushed her way to the register. Then she stopped. "Bring it up later tonight and we will open it together."

"Yeah. Yeah... At my pace. One thing at a time," Dee said.

"Dee, I'm not forcing you. I just thought it might be easier for you. I am just here for support. You call all the shots," Lizzy said. Then she spit in her hand stuck it out to shake with Dee. She laughed.

"Remember when you did that to me? Oh my God, that's when I knew I had your honesty. By the way, it is disgusting, but if that is what it takes...Shake," Lizzy demanded. So Dee spit and shook. They grinned at each other.

"Okay, now that we have decided to do this later, let me get home and rest a bit. I'll be back around closing," Dee said. She felt her tension easing. *It will be easier to do it with Lizzy by my side.*

"Promise?" Lizzy asked.

"Yep, I promise," Dee replied. She made her way to the hook, took down her back pack, and stopped a second. "What if I don't want to know what is in it?" she asked.

"But what if you do?" Lizzy sang out. "Think positive, Dee. You are the one that taught me that. I would always whine about finding Mr. Right. You said he would come along at the right time. Remember?" Lizzy smiled. "Go! Go rest! We could be here all night going through that chest."

"Better call Joe and tell him you may run late tonight and why. He might get worried," Dee added as she made her way to the door.

As she unlocked the door to her truck she felt a tinge of giddiness. *This is kinda exciting, like an adventure.* She cranked up the truck and backed it out of the parking space and headed to her house.

As she pulled into the drive she turned the truck off and sat for a minute. *What is so scary anyway? Gotta love that Lizzy, always makes me feel so much better about things.* She got out, headed into the house, went straight to her room and plopped down onto her bed and feel asleep instantly.

* * * * * *

*Dee slowly sat upright in the bed, then slowly stood. She felt light, light-headed you could say. Made her way to the chest, which still sat on the kitchen table, where she had left it early that morning. She glanced over her shoulder to her bed were she still slept. Looking at her empty shell... What is happening? Thought is all I am. Her mind was leading her soul to the chest. Only a foot closer and it would be within reach, but she was only thought - having no arms to open it frustrated her.*

*Dee was becoming frustrated the more she peered at the chest. Then in a flash, as if a light had come on, the chest opened. Out flew thousands of butterflies and bright snaps of light. Enchanting and magical, she floated closer to see what lay inside.*

*There in the bottom of the chest was a beautiful rose that looked as though it had just been picked from the garden. Alive. More alive than if it was still attached to the bush. That was all that it held. Confusion filled her head and a voice from behind her said, "The answer to your questions are in the chest."*

*The voice was familiar. A young boy's voice, full of innocence but tough as nails. Dee's mind turned to visualize the voice. It was Henry Jr., her older brother. Dee was so young when he had passed that she only had a vague recollection of him but she knew it was him. Her mother always had pictures of him all throughout the house, and it was him. There he stood bare foot in overalls that were too small. With a smile of mischief across his face, he said, "Dee, remember this... What you think it is... it really isn't." Henry's voice echoed as he faded.*

Dee suddenly sat up from her bed. She was back in her body and all was just as she had left it when she had fallen into bed. She sat for minutes trying to process what had happen. Then she looked over at the clock on her dresser, to see how long she had slept.

"Ah!" she yipped in surprise. There sat a little boy with his arms folded. A very silent, angry boy sat sulking on top of the dresser. *That isn't Henry. I just saw him. I know him!*

"Who are you?" she asked. The room was silent. "Who are you angry with?"

At that moment a noise came from the chest. *Thump, thump, thump.* Dee turned to look towards the chest. In that second, the boy disappeared.

She walked to the bathroom and splashed water on her face to wash away the dread that had settled on her again. "Dee, just get this over with," she said to her reflection in the mirror. She brushed her hair, changed into clean cloths, and then grabbed the chest. She marched her way to the truck.

Across the street at Johnny's shop, a light trickled from the garage. *He is working late.* Johnny appeared from underneath the car he was working on and glanced her way. He got to his feet.

"Hello, beautiful lady!" he hollered as he wiped his hands on a shop rag.

"Hey Johnny! We need to all get together one night when we aren't so busy!" Dee yelled back.

"Sure do! Been missing the old times!" He smiled. Then the smile slowly faded and he turned and walked inside the garage.

"I wonder what's bothering him?" *Even he is upset about having to be grown-up and take care of responsibilities all the time.*

"Ugggg...Where did time go?" Dee shouted, then cranked the truck and pulled away.

# CHAPTER EIGHTEEN
## The Chest

*Sometimes when things are falling apart, they may actually be falling into place.* **Unknown**

Lizzy wiped down the bar where two customers had just left, a man and a women who looked and acted as if they were having an affair. Lizzy never passed judgment or assumed, just watched.

Then she noticed Dee pulled into the parking space out front of BUCKETS. *She didn't chicken out. That's my Dee.* Lizzy giggled for a split second, but knew Dee would not take kindly to her amusement, so she quickly "serioused-up" before Dee walked into the bar.

"Hey," Lizzy said before Dee even made it completely through the door. "Did you bring it?" Lizzy asked noticing Dee was empty handed.

"Yes, but I left it out in the truck. I wanted to talk to you first and I didn't want it to hear," Dee whispered.

"Really Dee?"

Lizzy was not sure if she was serious or if something bad had happened. Dee had been acting quite unusual lately. First the obsessions with her things, then the horrible fear of the Jared-guy. Lizzy had to give her credit, she *was* right on the money with that one.

"Are you okay?" she asked, concerned for her friend.

Dee waved her hand. "I'm fine. After I left here, I went home and fell asleep. A deep, hard sleep. The kind you have that makes you feel frozen in place. At least your body is," she said as she went behind the bar to grab a soda. She decided she needed a beer instead.

"Oh yeah, I have had those. Like when you want to yell something in your dream and nothing comes out," Lizzy said totally understanding Dee.

"Exactly...But this was a little weirder." Dee took a sip. "I could see my body still asleep on the bed. I was out of my body, Lizzy!" Dee said and then swigged down the beer.

*Out of her body? Yep... She is stressed about the chest.* Lizzy made light of what Dee had just said. For one, she never *really* understood Dee's belief system. Accepted it, enjoyed learning it, but never quit grasped it. Lizzy straightened the stools at the bar.

"You don't have to do anything that you don't want to do, Dee. The chest can wait until you are ready."

"No! Now it has to happen! Tonight!" Dee took the last swig of beer and threw the bottle in the trash. "I am more than ready now."

She exhaled, then walked out from behind the bar, out to the truck and grabbed the chest and returned inside. She set it on top of the pool table and took two steps back and stared. *Thank God there are no customers left. They would think she'd gone mad.*

"It doesn't seem scary at all, Dee. Actually seems a bit enchanting. Was this yours as a little girl?" Lizzy asked as she stepped closer to it. Lizzy wiped her hand over the top to clean the dust from the sticker of Raggedy Ann's face. *Something beautiful and magical about this chest, not at all scary.*

"Yeah, I think so. My mother must have kept it for me to open at a later time. I do believe she is telling me... Now is the time," Dee said, still in a frozen state.

*Well...Is she going to open it or should I?* Lizzy turned and looked at Dee. Dee must have read her mind.

"I need to be the one to do this, Lizzy." Dee stepped forward...slowly unlatched the latch. Then she undid the straps that kept it sealed, and lifted the lid.

"Wow," Lizzy said as she glanced over top of Dee's shoulder.

The chest had two Indian ceramic pieces that looked as though they were hand painted. A dream catcher that had two hawk's feet intertwined in it and feathers that dangled from it. The feathers looked as though they were from the same hawk.

Lizzy nonchalantly looked a little closer. She could see a diary of some sort, with a tree imprinted on the top of it. Dee picked that up first. Ever so gently she rubbed her hand across its surface as if reading brail.

"This was my mothers," Dee whispered. At that very moment a dried rose fell from the book. It must have been pressed in the journal.

Dee opened it slowly. From what Lizzy could tell the dates started a year or so after Dee had been born. Lizzy didn't want to be too nosey. She also knew with Dee, she would talk when she needed to. Lizzy knew that eventually she could ask more questions, so she returned to looking in the chest as Dee stood staring at the journal. There were some old pictures laying at the bottom.

"Oh my God, Dee look at this," Lizzy blurted out as she pulled one of the pictures from the chest. It was the old house they were so fond of. The one that had housed the tavern owned by the two women who were friends of Lizzy's grandmother.

In the picture, the house looked a lot newer, the two women backs were turned in the picture and holding the hand of a little boy who also had his back turned as well. "My grandmother never mentioned a little boy," Lizzy acknowledged.

The picture mesmerized the two of them for what was merely minutes but seemed much longer. Quickly Dee put everything back in the chest and closed the lid. Lizzy thought that Dee was scared *again*.

"Okay, I did it! I still need to take this slow, Lizzy," Dee said. She picked up the chest and marched it out to the truck.

Lizzy stood in silence, still not sure of what had just happened. *Whatever it is that is bothering that girl, I need to let her know I am here.* Dee returned through the front door.

"Dee whatever it is... *please*... Just know I am here for you. Okay? You don't need to face this stuff alone," Lizzy said fearing Dee was on the verge of a break down.

"I know Liz, I just need to take it slow. My mind is playing tricks on me. If I think each step through... I will be fine." Dee hugged Lizzy and turned to leave.

Before she got out the door, she turned and gave Lizzy a sad smile.

"Unfortunately this is something I do need to do *alone*."

## CHAPTER NINETEEN
### Love What You Do


**Humor is the great thing, the saving thing. The minute it crops up, all our irritation and resentments slip away, and a sunny spirit takes their place. Mark Twain**


Dee slowly pulled the truck into the driveway of her home, still shocked about the picture of the old house and the little boy. Thoughts bobbled through her head.

*I have a connection to that house. I always loved it and the story behind it. But who is the little boy? Is he the same angry boy that was on my dresser? Why is he so angry?*

Dee opened the truck door and stepped out as her thoughts bounced around. She noticed the light on in the garage across the street. *Johnny is still working?* She decided to take a break from her crazy thoughts and chat with him.

As she walked into the garage she saw Johnny sitting on tires stacked in the corner, *drinking* a beer.

"Hey, I thought you quit?" Dee asked with a quick nod at the can he was holding.

"I just thought one would actually do me some good tonight." Johnny took a swig, stood, and tossed it into a barrel just outside the door.

"How do you and Lizzy do it, Dee? How do you stay sane after doing all the work it takes to own a business? Not to mention the paperwork, the long hours. Then it's like there is no time to socialize or have fun anymore."

"Well Johnny, it *is* a lot. Lizzy and I had this same conversation not too long ago. Honestly? You have to weigh out what means more to you. Have to find some balance, I guess. If you feel like something's missing... look for it," Dee said as she fumbled through the tool box.

"Hell, chasing butterflies is something everyone needs to do. Lizzy and I chased butterflies for years. We found where we need to be." She smiled. "Johnny, look at the metaphor of a butterfly—it means change. You *need* change."

She turned to face him. "You've been in business now for two years, right? The newness is gone for you. Add on some help, or even close up one extra day. Something to get you out of your routine." Silence filled the garage as she continued to rummage through the mechanic's treasures.

"Thanks Dee, you know you're right," Johnny said, snapping Dee to attention. "Armadilla huntin' was more a hobby than anything else and I got *paid* to do it. Hmmmm, love what you do," he murmured as if a light had gone off in his head.

"You love working on cars. So embrace your work and then it will embrace you. Just because you captured *this* butterfly doesn't mean you can't catch another." Dee smiled.

"That is exactly what I need to do. I am always so worried about making the money to pay the bills, I don't get pleasure from it anymore," Johnny concurred.

"It isn't what is happening, it's how you *feel* about what's happening." Dee walked over and hugged her old friend. "I've gotta get some sleep. Remember—positive thinking!"

She walked away with a slight smile on her lips, humming a familiar tune. When she reached her front door she remembered the chest and then decided it could stay outside for the night.

About that time she heard a loud BANG come from Johnny's garage. He came running out and yelled, "Damn you, Dee! It's on!"

Dee giggled as she entered the house. Yep, the battle of the pranks was back on in full force. Now he's on even ground.

*He just missed me, that's all.*

## CHAPTER TWENTY
### The Journal

**Youth fades; love droops, the leaves of friendship fall; A mother's secret hope outlives them all. Oliver Wendell Holmes**

Cooler air lurched around the corner not allowing the town a chance to notice. Dee's eyes fluttered a few times before she realized she'd fallen asleep after tossing and turning to do so. She had actually gotten a good night's sleep with no crazy nightmares.

She always woke in a good mood and that was something that made Lizzy crazy. She threw the covers off and sat forward to review her dreams like Dr. Renee had suggested in the past. *No bad dreams last night. Hmmm... It's a good start for today. Maybe I will read one of my mother's journal entries.*

"Dee, one step at a time," she said to herself as she got to her feet. She proceeded to the kitchen and thought back to a time when she was a young girl. Her mother always made her a sippy cup of hot cocoa during the cold seasons. *That's what I would like to have this morning.*

After whipping up a steaming creamy hot cocoa she placed it on the table and headed out to her truck to get the journal. *The chest is staying here.* The chest had been in Dee's truck for weeks now.

She removed the journal, rubbing her hand over top of the journal as if it was alive and needed love. She walked back through the screen door and sat at the kitchen table staring at the journal. She took a sip of her cocoa and proceeded to open the journal to the first page.

A letter fell from the book as it opened. It was dated and postmarked two years after Dee was born. Dee gently tucked it into the back of the book.

"One thing at a time, Dee," she whispered to herself. She started to read the entry.

*July 29, 1975*

> *Today is my first entry. I have discovered I am with child. Dee will be blessed with another sibling. Henry Jr.'s death has been something that has devastated all of us. Dee still walks the house calling his name. She plays in his room as though he is there. I worry she may be faced with her father's sickness. By the grace of god, I've been blessed with another child in my womb. Things here have been quite scary trying to face them alone. I sometimes get angry with myself for ever leaving the reservation. We had unity there, at least I should have fought to stay. Henry senior believed we no longer need to be at the reservation and decided for us. The reservation was good for him. It made him whole and at peace. Henry Senior has been gone now for one month,*

*and I am afraid he may never return. He will never meet his unborn child or even know this baby exists. He is a sick man and I hope he finds a cure in his searches. Today I decided to start a journal in hopes of someday revealing the truths of all that has happened. Also to teach my children of their father, which they may never get to know.*

*August 1, 1975*

*Henry Bishop's possessions were those of a kind gentle man. Never feared hard work and never wanted a thing from anyone. Although he was not of American-Indian decent he lived as though he was. At the age of 21, I met him on a Seminole Indian reservation while I was doing internship for my degree in Historical science. He was truly an amazing man. He held great responsibility to the tribe and was honored among them. His only fault was he believed a curse had been placed upon his family centuries ago. Many believed he had a sickness, but it was more than that. He, as the psychologist would consider, was a schizophrenic. He would tell of the voices that spoke to him. He even mentioned one kind voice told him he would marry me. At that time I just laughed, and enjoyed the moment. Years later we had been spiritually married by the reservation's shaman. I often doubted the voices, but never truly dis-believed*

*either. Today I cry inside for him, because
I do believe he was a sick man. He often
would speak of the angels guiding him.
Today I pray that they are.*

Aug. 19, 1975

*My children need to know that Henry
Bishop truly loved them. He believed if he
was no longer around, that we would live a
long life. He would tell me of days that
these voices were of the light. Later he
would say darkness was trying to obstruct
his view. He was a man that tried every
known practice of belief, in hopes one day
finding the one that worked. I myself, never
understood the obsession he had with it
all. After we left the reservation, we moved
to the small town where I had grown up.
We found our home to start a family, a
family he feared he would lose. He seemed
strange to the locals here, but they never
understood him as I did. After Henry Jr.'s
death, he became even more eccentric, and
one day he was gone.*

"He just up and left her?" Dee shouted, slamming the journal shut. *He doesn't even know Gina was born?* Dee rubbed her hand over top of the page.

*My mother feared that I may also have this... so-called sickness.* She could hear her mother's voice in every word she read. She could smell her as if she was there with her. Her mother's essence caressed the top of her shoulder with a gentle touch. Dee turned to look.

Her mother waited in a white flowing sun dress, holding a rose. The ghostly figure reached out to hand her the rose and in a soft whisper said, "You are not sick. Nor is he. Go and find your father, he needs you." The beautiful essence faded into the sound of the whisper.

Dee stood and quickly wiped the tear that had fallen from her face. *Tuff as nails. Hunh?*

Dee never embraced emotion especially when it was hers. She always had more compassion for others than she did for herself. She would numb herself, just as she had done as a child. She so badly missed her mother and her family. She needed to find her father.

*Maybe Lizzy is right, we need to get up with the times. I'll go see what one of those fancy computers cost. They say the phone company can hook it up to the World Wide Web and find anyone. If my dad is out there, that's how I'm going to find him.*

She went to her room to dress, then made her way to the garden to set the timer for watering. She knew she was going to have a busy day. *I'll see if Lizzy will come over tonight. She'll show me how to work the computer. God knows I'm no good at that technology stuff.* She pulled a few weeds from the garden and then glanced over at the swing. That damn cockle plant had sprouted back, the only plant thriving in the cooler weather.

*I will not allow you to take over my garden.* She grabbed the small hand shovel and scooped it up and marched it to the fire pit. "I'll take care of you later," she said to the plant as she tossed it into the pit. She went back in through the screen door, washed her hands and headed out to her truck to go find a fancy computer.

"Hey, Miss Dee!" Johnny hollered with a smirk.

"Hi, Johnny," Dee yelled back sensing that a prank might be coming soon. *Oh boy, what's that fellah gonna try doing to me? It's been weeks and nothing...*

She smiled and cautiously entered her truck. As she cranked it, she listened. *No boom.* Back in the day, she and Johnny tried every prank possible on each other. *We're seasoned now, so what will be in store? He's making me want to relax before he try's something.*

Dee pulled the truck away and headed to the next town north. Department stores, like Sears, flooded that town. There was talk in town that a store called Wal-mart was opening within the next year. But Dee needed a computer now, especially if she planned on finding her dad on that web thing.

## CHAPTER TWENTY-ONE
### Flat Tire

**"With the new day comes new strength and new thought." Eleanor Roosevelt**

Hours later, Dee had been to five different stores to compare prices on computers. She finally found what she thought she might be looking for. Driving down the interstate there was a sudden lull on the truck.

An awful sound came from the back left tire. Yep, she had a flat tire all right. She pulled the truck to the side of the road and got out to check.

"Damn it. Brand new truck and I get a flat tire," Dee huffed. She got out the spare and the jack. She was darn lucky it was a new truck, because she had everything she needed to fix a flat. At least it was the first car she'd ever had that came with a spare. As she unscrewed the lug nuts she thought again about Lizzy's car phone idea.

*Once I get the spare on ...I'll stop at the next pay phone and give Lizzy a call. Tell her to check on me in a bit to see if I make it back with this donut tire. I'll see if she can come by after work....*

"Guess maybe Lizzy is right, one of those car phones would come in handy right now," Dee huffed aloud.

Exhausted from the last turn of the lug nut, she placed the flat in the back of the truck, hopped back into the truck and jumped back on the interstate. Carefully she exited at the next available exit. She found a pay phone at the first gas station she came to.

She poked a quarter and a dime into the slot and dialed. Lizzy answered on the third ring.

"Hey Lizzy, it's Dee. Will you call the house in about twenty minutes to make sure I make it back home? I got a flat. This spare is a donut, no bigger than a bicycle tire. Are you going to be busy after work today?" Dee asked.

"Not that I can think of. Yeah, sure I'll call. Were you wanting to go through that chest some more?" Lizzy's voice traveled through the receiver.

"No... Still taking some time with that, I know it has been a while... I bought a computer," Dee said. The chattering of customers was all she heard. "I thought you could show me how to work the darn thing."

"Sure, why did you buy a computer?"

Dee knew Lizzy would be confused. Lizzy was the computer person, not Dee. Lizzy knew computers well. She first started working on computers when she was in college, and again after BUCKETS first opened. She was always talking about the latest stuff out.

"I'll explain why I did this when I see you. But the guy said it was the best out there and had a lot of memory. He said I could even get onto the World Wide Web with it." Dee said.

"I'll try to help Dee, but that is new area for me too. I think you need to get a hold of the phone company. Get what they call dial up Internet service installed at your house first. Wow Dee, you really want to get up with the times," Lizzy's giggle echoed.

"Yeah, well, I think we should look into those car phones that you mentioned, too. I am at a pay phone right now." Dee laughed as she glanced around the gas station.

"See Dee? Instinct. I knew we could use a car phone." Lizzy giggled again. "Ok, see you at six thirty. I need to give Joe a call and let him know my plans. Love ya girl."

"Okay, six thirty, see you then. Don't forget to ring me at the house in fifteen to twenty minutes. Ok?"

Dee hung the pay phone up and returned to her truck. She couldn't do much about the tire that was flat, but she knew Johnny would be able to fix it or get her another one. Slowly she made her way back home. The donut tire was doing the job, but she sure didn't want to risk going too fast with it.

She pulled into the driveway of her house and stepped out of the truck. Johnny looked out of the garage and slowly appeared into sunlight. He smiled and wiped his hands on a shop rag.

"Johnny, I think I have a hole in my tire. I think it needs a patch. I didn't notice damage so I think it should be fixable," Dee yelled to him as he laughed and stared at her spare tire.

"Gosh Dee, I got to hand it to ya... I thought for sure you would have called me minutes after you left to come help you. You did it, all on your own." Johnny looked concerned. "I'm sorry. Your tire is fine, I let the air out of it this morning. It was a 'Gotcha!' but looks as though it didn't get ya. I really need to work on some safer pranks." Johnny scratched his head. "I think you are still one up on me. I'll get to the tire ASAP, promise!" He returned to the garage shaking his head in disbelief.

"Damn, I am good," she announced with a sense of pride. *Obstacles may slow me down but I will always shine in the end.*

"Ha-Ha-Ha!" Dee laughed her best evil laugh. She grabbed the computer from the truck and glanced at the chest that still sat in the passenger seat. "You are going to have to wait some more. I've got to find my dad."

Dee proceeded into the house with her arms full with her new computer. She set it down on the coffee table in the living room and contemplated where it would have to go. She noticed a phone line in the corner of the room.

"I'll move my mom's old desk out here and set up there. It will fit perfectly."

She made her way to the phone and called the phone company. They actually said they would send someone within the next three hours which was perfect for Dee because Lizzy would arrive there soon after. Then the phone rang and Dee hoped it wasn't the phone company with a problem. She grinned when she heard Lizzy's voice.

"Yep, I'm here. Phone Company can make it out today to hook up the Internet. So I'm in."

Lizzy assured Dee she'd be there by six-thirty, then hung up amidst the chatter of the bar.

After moving the desk, Dee unpacked the computer and set it up, exactly how the guy at the store explained. When she finished, she flopped down on the couch and drifted off to sleep.

* * * * * *

*Darkness covered her; damp, mud-like material. She desperately wiped it from her eyes in an attempt to see. Nothing. Just darkness, cold and damp. She strained to see and slowly made out an outline of a small boy sitting Indian style in the mud. Her eyes adjusted to the darkness and she was able to make out the figure. It was the angry boy she had seen days before, sitting on top of her dresser. His arms were folded and he squinted at her, his bottom lip poked out as if he was pouting.*

*She tried to speak to him but no sound came from her mouth. She tried harder. This time sound came from her mouth, but it wasn't in the form of language. It sounded more like a tone. She desperately tried again. The sound bellowed like a fog horn and made her jump.*

Dee sat up quickly to a knock at the front door. She was awake and her heart pounded something fierce. She stood and answered the door. It was the worker from the phone company. She glanced at the time and realized she had slept for nearly an hour. *Didn't have any nightmares last night, but of course I had to have one today. Right now!*

She let the guy in and tried to calm herself so he didn't think she was crazy. She watched as he fumbled with the telephone lines. Then he stood and showed her how to get on-line. He also explained it would take a few minute to dial up.

After the BellSouth worker finished, she walked him out. After closing the door, she turned and leaned her back against the door and exhaled.

Shuffling to the kitchen, she continued to calm herself. "I am going to make myself a cup of tea. Lizzy's fairytale tea to be exact. Maybe that will calm my nerves."

## CHAPTER TWENTY-TWO
### Crazy Girl

**Remember, I am with you always. Matthew 28:20**

Lizzy looked up from the register as the front door opened. Gracey was running late.

"Hey...I did your register and stocked you up for tonight," Lizzy said as she met Gracey at the end of the bar.

"Great. Sorry I'm late. Harry's car broke down and he needed a ride." Gracey hung her purse on the coat hook.

"No biggie. I'm going to Dee's to help her with the new computer she got today," she told Gracey.

"A computer? That is *so* not Dee,"Gracey said with a shake of her head.

Lizzy nodded. "I know. That's what worries me."

"She has been quite distracted lately. Almost as if she's in her own world," Gracey said.

"Dee is *always* in her own world and it's usually a happy one. Lately she seems terrified in it and that is what concerns me the most," Lizzy babbled as she started to leave. Then she paused a moment.

"Gracey, thank you for everything you do for us. If we didn't have you, things probably would be a lot harder for us. I don't mean just here at BUCKETS, either." She gave Gracey a quick hug, grabbed her purse and dashed out through the door.

She made her way to her daddy's Jeep. Yep, Lizzy was still driving that old thing and it still ran good. Lizzy of course, had bought it off her daddy a few years back. That was a fight itself, to get him to take the money, but Lizzy had finally won the battle.

Now the battle was for Dee to be happy and come to terms with whatever was gnawing at her.

Lizzy thought back to the years she was alone and how she struggled daily with her loneliness. *They may have been painful, but I learned the most about life and myself in those days. If Dee wouldn't have been there for me, I don't know what I would have done. So tonight, and any night after, I will be there for her. As long as she needs me. I will be there.*

Not conscious of it, Lizzy had driven all the way to Dee's house. She pulled into the drive right behind Dee's truck and parked. She stared at the house and then at the garden she so fondly remembered. A smile slowly spread across her face. *Good times.*

She got out of the Jeep and heard Johnny from across the street.

"Hey, pretty lady! How is Joe?" he asked.

"He's good, Johnny. I'll tell him you said hello." Lizzy waved and continued towards the house. *I'm sure Johnny's been keeping an eye on Dee.* Lizzy the Worrier was more concerned for Dee than she would let on to anyone.

She knocked a few times on the door. No answer. That was a fear she'd fought with for years. Something horrible behind a door with no answer. She turned the knob and peaked her head in. The whisk of cooler air chilled her. She wrapped her sweater snug to her body.

"Hello? Dee?" Lizzy yelled inside.

She smelled something burning. She noticed smoke coming from the back yard and followed it around to the back of the house. There Dee stood next to the fire pit.

"Here you are." Lizzy paced, relieved that Dee was all right, the oak leaves crunching beneath her feet.

"Hey. I didn't hear you pull up. Just getting rid of some nasty weeds I've had. They keep coming back in my garden." Dee stared deeply into the fire.

"I see that. *All* of that is weeds?" Lizzy noticed the large pile in the pit. She and Dee never had more than a couple of handfuls a week. Even when they got behind the pile never amounted to that much.

"There was not that much this morning—they seemed to have doubled while I was gone today," Dee said, again still staring as if the fire had her in a trance.

"Come on, I want to check out that new computer of yours." Lizzy tugged on Dee's shirt to snap her out of her stare.

"Yeah, yeah. I want to find my dad on that World Wide Web." Dee turned with a smile.

Lizzy stopped in her tracks. "Are you okay?"

"I'm fine. I'll explain later. Just not ready to talk about it yet. I want to work it out in *my* head first," Dee added with a bright smile.

They walked towards the house in silence. As they approached the wooden screen door Dee spoke. "I read some of my mother's journal this morning."

"You did?" Lizzy stopped again. "Now that's a step closer. You are doing good, Dee. Take it inch by inch." She entered the house when Dee held the screen door open for her. "Did you find what you've been looking for?" Lizzy asked.

"Well...my Dad *may* have been a schizophrenic." Dee smiled a fake smile, which she was getting very good at.

"My mother, from what I did read, feared that I may have the same sickness." Dee stopped with her back to Lizzy in front of the desk were the computer sat.

Lizzy glanced around the house that seemed a bit untidy, which was also unlike Dee.

Lizzy rubbed her arms to settle the chill that had crawled up them and said, "It is freezing in here, Dee. Is your heat working?"

"I know..." Dee whispered with a fearful look. "The heat is working fine. It's them..."

*Oh dear she needs me more than I thought.* Trying not to look too concerned, Lizzy grabbed Dee by her shoulders and looked her in the eyes.

"Dee, you are a good person. No matter what you learn about your father, your childhood or even things that you thought were... but find out they aren't. As long as you know... You. Are. A. Good. Person. Know who you are... You can conquer anything." Lizzy let go of Dee's shoulders and felt empathy for her dearest friend.

She knew when Dee fell, which was very rare, she fell hard. At least after Raymond's death she had. That was a fear that haunted Lizzy, every day. *She is a stronger person now. With so much to live for. Please God help me say the right things to her.*

"Dee, we will do this... All of this, together. Okay? But you are going to have to talk to me about it. I don't want to pry, but I won't know what you are up against if you don't talk to me about it."

"I hear their voices, Lizzy," Dee said blankly. "I see people that have died. Just like that crap they used to say about me in high school. I *am* that crazy girl." Dee glared down at her feet in shame.

Silence stood between them, separating them for a split second.

Lizzy folded her arms in front of her. "That's not exactly news, Dee. Besides... *now* you want to worry about what others think? I love you and you are a good person. Let's find your dad. Maybe he has some answers for us."

Lizzy sat at the computer desk and noticed Dee had placed a picture of her mother beside the computer screen. She thought hard to herself. *If Dee is hearing voices... please help her hear the right ones.* She gave the picture another glance as if asking Dee's mother to be there for her.

Dee stood behind Lizzy as they searched on the World Wide Web for the family tree of Henry Bishop, Sr.

## CHAPTER TWENTY-THREE
### Deidra Marie

**The most beautiful things in the world cannot be seen or even touched; they must be felt with the heart. Helen Keller**

After hours of searching through the Web, Lizzy stood and stretched. Dee sat down in the desk chair and stared at the computer screen as if her dad was going to suddenly pop out. No luck there.

"Dee, there are at least a hundred-thousand Henry Bishops out there. This is going to take time. I am exhausted and Joe is probably wondering what is taking me so long." Lizzy yawned loudly as she stretched some more.

"I know... we'll do this another night," Dee said as she spun around on the desk chair. "I was just hoping we would get *something. Anything.*"

"I know you were." Lizzy placed her hand on Dee's shoulder. "Look, you need rest. BUCKETS isn't going to open itself tomorrow, and I *don't* want to do a double." Lizzy winked and grabbed her purse from the couch, slinging it over her shoulder.

"Get some rest," Lizzy ordered as she fished her keys from her purse. She headed to the door, opened it and then turned to Dee. "You know, I don't think you're 'that crazy girl' or 'sick'. So quit thinking that way. You've got a lot going on, but you're not nuts."

Dee nodded and stood. "Thanks, Lizzy. That is exactly what I needed to hear." She walked to Lizzy and hugged her. "Get home before Joe sends the swat team out after you."

After Lizzy's headlights disappeared from the driveway, Dee walked over to the journal that sat on the kitchen table. She rubbed her hand across the top and heard the sound of her mother calling her name. *"Dee Marie..."*

Dee picked up the journal and starting reading it again...

*Aug.30, 1975*

*Today Dee has asked where her Dada is. I only wish I knew. I keep saying to her he is with Henry Jr., with God. Truth is I often wonder if he is still alive. Months have passed and I haven't gotten any word from him. Henry Bishop was a man that would turn to the bottle when the voices got too strong for him to bear. That all must have started at a young age. Although I never met her, he often spoke of the Aunt that had raised him. Deidra Marie Bishop. She was the women Dee is named after. She never married and took in many people just as she raised Henry. She owned a house southwest of town, which she turned into a tavern. Henry had lost his parents at the age of seven, and she had taken him in. Henry would describe her as an eccentric woman and often spoke of his aunt's friend Lizette. She was a friend his aunt had taken in after the tragic death of her husband in the war. Together the women opened the tavern. They live on the second floor of the home, which had become the town tavern. Henry often spoke of sneaking downstairs after everyone had gone home, and sipping on the bottles of whiskey. Of course, his Aunt never knew. He would say he did it to make the voices he heard stop, but years later he learned it only made the darkness even darker. This baby I am holding in my womb has started to move which brings great joy to my heart, but sadness too. I suppose that Henry's voices are probably no different than my own consciousness of joy and sadness. I pray for him every night. He is a good man, and he needs to see that the light of God still shines in him.*

"The connection to the old house... and the women...and the picture with the little boy. It makes sense to me now," Dee said as she closed the journal. She hugged it to her chest and closed her eyes. *That is why... I've always loved that story. Lizzy's grandma knew them and my mother. Lizzy and I were destined to meet. History always repeats itself.*

Dee opened her eyes, then stood. She put the journal down on the table. Still baffled about the idea of history repeating itself, yet knowing she was at least partially right, she glanced at her mother's picture on the desk in the living room.

She smiled as she walked to the bathroom and got ready for bed. She slowly strolled to her room and slid under the covers. Still wondering about all the curious parallels; how she had come to love that story of the tavern; how she too, owned a bar. *I was named after her, Deidra Marie Bishop.* Sleep arrived quickly.

*She slowly crossed over the rail road tracks. Her bare feet ached from walking on the stones. She walked the smoother dirt path that lead to the house where the large oak stood.*

*A forest stood behind the old house as if guarding it from the world. Tree roots pushed the stepping stones up from the ground. She placed her bare foot on the first step. Her flowing white sun dress, just like the one her mother had worn, flapped from the gentle breeze.*

*She continued into the old house and was surrounded by music and the sounds of people chattering, but no one was there. Slowly moving up the staircase, she reached the top of the stairs and stood in the second floor hallway. The hallway slowly extended itself with each step she took. A trunk sat at the far end of the hall, but with each step, the further away it seemed to be. As she stepped each bare foot onto the creaking hardwood floor, a sense of secrets and mystery surrounded her.*

Dee woke to the sound of her alarm clock buzzing. She sat up to reflect on her dream. Then made her way to her dresser to turn the alarm off.

As she brought her hand up to the clock, she almost jumped back a foot. There he sat, the angry boy she'd encountered before, arms folded and lip poked out.

"Who are you? Who are you mad at?" she asked.

His reply was to fade away as if he was never there.

## CHAPTER TWENTY-FOUR
### Children at Play


**For in every adult there dwells the child that was, and in every child there lies the adult that will be. John Connolly, The Book of Lost Things**


On Saturday, Dee woke early to tend the garden and shower before Lizzy and Joe came by to pick her up.

They planned to ride together to attend Lindsey's birthday party. Dee took a peak out the window to see if they had arrived yet. *Maybe I'll have a few minutes to read one of my mother's journal entries.*

She darted into the kitchen where the book waited on the table to tell her more of her father. God knows the World Wide Web is a hay stack I don't have time for. So she sat for a moment opened the journal and read.


*Sept. 22, 1975*
*Fall is in the air. You can smell the cooler weather starting to approach. The leaves are starting to fall and Dee is outside rolling around in them. She is a happy child and she is starting*

*to notice that my belly is growing larger daily. She is excited about being a big sister. She said to me yesterday that Dada and Henry Jr. are going to be sad they missed the new baby. Which made me realize something, the memories of spending time with a loved one, is more important than never having them in your life. I may have only had Henry Sr. and Henry Jr. grace me with their love for a short time, but I wouldn't trade it for anything else imaginable. I am thankful for what time I did have with them. I will forgive my angry heart for wanting more. Dee is my child. I shall teach her how to appreciate the precious lives we are given, that she too has taught me. Dee is very much like her father, in more ways than she will ever know. So today I vow to keep her faith in God's light, so she will never feel the curse Henry Sr. believed was placed onto his family. Stay in your happy place, sweet Dee. Never leave your garden, and roll in the leaves of life. May they comfort you in every way. The cold winter will only be a season and the spring sun will shine upon your soul once again.*

Out of the journal pages Henry Jr.'s Epitaph fell onto her lap. Dee picked it up and read the clipping.

*Henry Daniel Bishop Jr. born Aug. 1, 1971-May 29, 1975*
*Beloved son of Henry Bishop and Dorothy Bishop*
*May God cradle you as we did the day you were born.*
*May he fulfill all your needs, as you so warmly deserve.*
*Rest my child, we will see you again.*
*Our work is not finished here to receive our reward.*
*Your time with us was short, but ever so grand.*
*You are our angel as God had planned.*

Dee slipped the clipping into the pages, closed the journal and placed it back onto the table. There was a knock at the door.

"Come in," she yelled as she stood. Joe poked his head in the door.

"You ready?" he asked.

"Yeah...," Dee blew her nose in a tissue to hide the fact she was starting to cry. "Where's Lizzy?" she asked through the tissue.

"Where do you think?" he said rolling his eyes. "She's spinning around like Mary Poppins out in your garden." He laughed.

Dee peeked out the window. Sure enough, she was out in the garden acting out some Cinderella scene and singing what sounded like one of the tunes—something about a Prince Charming.

"I worry about that girl sometimes, Dee," Joe said opening the door for Dee.

"No worries, Joe. It's all good," Dee said smiling as they watched Lizzy twirl about.

"Are you ready?" Lizzy asked in a sing song way and fluttered herself in their direction like an oversized fairy.

The three slung their arms around each other and headed for the car. Dee squeezed into the back of the hot rod and noticed Joe had finally finished the work on the interior.

"Wow Joe, it looks great in here!"

"Yeah it does, but I think I might trade it in for a better car for Lizzy. She can't be lugging a child around in that old Jeep," he stated.

Lizzy rolled her eyes. "I'm not pregnant yet. Well as far as we *know*, I'm not."

Dee just sat in the back and watched the two communicate and snickered to herself. They were a sight. She thought back to the time that Lizzy revealed to her that she had the "hots" for Joe, then snickered some more. *We have all come a long way.*

They finally arrived at Ripley's home. Children scattered throughout the front yard, darting in and out from the birch tree that stood as shade. Ripley huddled in the center of the children in an attempt to get their attention.

She gave a quick wave Hello as Dee, Lizzy and Joe unloaded from the car. Lizzy looked mesmerized by the site of the munchkins with their runny noses and all. *I sure hope a child is what Lizzy wants. Today will be the test.* Dee chuckled as she grabbed the gift from the back seat.

This is going to be some party, Dee thought to herself as she watched Ripley who tried to explain how to pin the tail on the donkey as the children were chasing each other and flip flopping onto the grass. Dee could see Ripley's frustration to make the party as perfect as possible. Ripley always wanted perfection for Lindsey. *I guess having this many kids at a party squashes the perfection idea. Doesn't look like perfection is in the works for today's party.*

Dee chuckled to herself as she sat down at the table. The table cloth matched the cake, balloons, and gift bags that Lizzy graciously admired. Dee could see the excitement that Lizzy and Joe shared as they watched the kids run about. It was almost as if they were trying it on for the day. Dee glanced over to the table next to her, and noticed Walter watching the shenanigans with a smile on his face. She thought back again to the time Ripley was so excited about dating the new hottie in town, which was Walter. She chuckled to herself again. *We were so young and happy.*

"Look how cute Lindsey is," Lizzy said to Dee. "We were there when she was born," Lizzy bragged to Joe with a wink.

"I can't believe she is six years old already," Dee added then glanced again at Walter, who had risen from his seat to meet Lindsey half way across the grass with a giant hug. Dee missed not having her father in her life. She was determined to keep looking. She needed to have memories of him. Dee may have missed it in her childhood, but was determined to get it now.

"Hey guys, so sorry I can't chat, kids are everywhere," Ripley gushed as she dashed by, heading towards the kids.

"I just love that dress Lindsey is wearing," Lizzy yelled to Ripley.

"I knew you would," Ripley called back as two of the kids bombarded her with questions.

Dee knew Lizzy loved all the girly stuff and was probably hoping to have a girl when the time came for her. *Lizzy is really serious about this baby stuff. We should probably consider hiring some more help, soon.*

The party was a great success, even if it didn't go exactly as Ripley had planned. To Dee it seemed as though Ripley was accepting the fact that perfection and children was almost a nearly impossible mission.

Dee knew Lizzy and Joe probably went home to work hard on trying to make that baby they so desperately wanted.

She went home to her garden and thought back to her childhood with greater appreciation, thankful for her mother, who gave her the best childhood she could have ever imagined.

## CHAPTER TWENTY-FIVE
### Alone on the Holidays

**Ye are all the children of light, and the children of the day: we are not of the night, nor of darkness. 1 Thessalonians 5:5**

Dee started her daily routine with her tea first, tending the garden, then getting washed up to open BUCKETS.

BUCKETS Halloween costume party was a big kick off to the holidays. Thanksgiving, Christmas, and New Year's celebrations came and went, complete with all of the chaos and extra work it took to decorate and cook special holiday foods.

Each holiday Dee spent alone in her home when she wasn't working. She avoided everyone and made excuses to not attend any personal holiday parties. She embraced her solitude, at least, she managed to avoid any living beings. She learned more from the journal. She rationalized and pulled the positive from everything she learned. If the slightest bit of darkness entered her mind she would rid it before it overwhelmed her.

She believed her time alone was teaching her to love herself and not need others to fulfill her happiness. If she could become happy with her own being, then any others would be a gift. And her love would be given unconditionally.

Dee finally started *feeling* a hair more positive. She took a moment to realize that it had been some time since she had allowed any darkness in her thoughts. She smiled today at the woman in the mirror.

Even though the angry boy was still showing up in her dreams or whatever they were, he didn't seem all that harmful- at least at the moment. Too bad that he seemed intent on frightening her.

Dee wasn't struggling any more with the idea of reading from her mother's journal, because it seemed to give her more information than the whole World Wide Web ever did. She decided to take her few spare minutes to finally remove the chest from the truck and tuck it in the house.

Yep, it had been there for months now. It was probably past time. *Positive thinking, Dee.* Her dread of the chest seemed to have subsided too.

She gave reading her mother's diary credit for that. *My mother would never allow me to be harmed. If anything is going to harm me, it will be me and my negative thinking.* That thought felt right and when she felt things were right, they usually were. *Instinct, go with the gut, Dee.*

She walked outside to get the chest from the truck. Johnny was standing by the back left tire.

"Hey, looks like that tire is still holding up for ya," Johnny said kicking at the tire he fixed months back with a curious smile. Dee thought he looked a little saddened by the fact he was losing his knack for pranks.

"Sure is," she said.

Johnny moved his way to the back of the truck and stopped just short of the tail gate as Dee pulled the chest from the front seat.

"Whatca got there?" he asked.

"A chest. It's a chest I had as a little girl. My mother put it up in the attic years ago." Dee stopped and exhaled and looked at Johnny.

"It's full of wonderful things, things I never knew about my childhood. Some things about my dad. I've been hauling it around for months now." Dee laughed. "It's time to check it out. It's sure to be what I've been needing to get me out of my funk."

"Wow, that sounds pretty magical, Dee," Johnny winked.

"Yes, magical it shall be." Dee nodded, turned, and headed for the door. Johnny trotted over to open the screen for her, a smirk still fixed on his face.

"Thanks again, Johnny!" she yelled as the screen door slammed behind her.

"You're welcome!" he chuckled as he returned across the street to the garage.

Dee dropped off the trunk, locked the house, went back outside and climbed into her truck, cranked it up and slowly backed out of the driveway. On route to work, she noticed cars kept beeping and waving at her, everyone smiling.

She turned into the parking lot of BUCKETS. A pickup truck with two teenage boys pulled up behind her and rolled down their window. That's one of the Erickson boys, she thought. *What does he want?*

"I like your sign," he smiled and they pulled away laughing. *My sign?* Dee looked up at the new *BUCKETS* sign across the top of the entrance of the bar. *It looks fine to me. What are they talking about?*

At that very moment, she realized that Johnny was acting quite weird. Uh oh! *Johnny!* He was waiting to see me relax, she thought.

She got out, walked around and looked at her tail gate that bore a giant sign that stretched from one side to the other; a sign that read, "Honk if you are HORNEY!"

She peeled it off, shaking her head. "Damn you, Johnny!" *He got me. He sure got me.*

How many cars *had* honked? She wondered. She took a few minutes to get over her embarrassment, then she made her way to the front door, key in hand.

A tall shadow fell across her feet. "Howdy ma'am. By any chance you know where to get a cold liquid beverage?" His southern drawl was very heavy, even stronger than Johnny's and his was pretty strong.

The man stood behind Dee wearing a giant ten gallon cowboy hat. Dee turned and looked up because he *was* tall. Abnormally tall.

"Sure do. Follow me," she said with a smile, as she turned the key. She flipped on lights as she made her way behind the bar. "What-cha having?" she asked as she tossed a coaster in front of him.

"Ice cold beer sounds purdy darn good right now," he drawled. Dee fought a laugh. When he said "ice" it sounded more like "ace."

"You got it." She reached into the cooler. "Where ya from?" She asked as she popped open a cold beer and placed it on the coaster.

"Texas. Just moved here bout week go," he said, then sipped his beer. He looked at the bottle. "Damn, that hit the spot."

"What made you move this way, from Texas?" Dee asked.

"Well we had to, me and the family. Property that was handed down to me from four generations got ruined when the oil companies started doing that fracking crap. Done poisoned my family's drinking supply. So I sold to start over, I guess." He took another sip of his beer then continued. "I'm purdy darn lucky. Some them families still staying on the properties, tryin' to fight to keep it. Them kids of theirs are sick and gettin sicker," he said as though he had a wad of bubble gum in his mouth. "Not my kids, I'm gonna make sure they healthy."

"How sad."

Dee, right at that moment, saw clearer as to why her father had left them. It all made sense. *He left us, because he believed*

She smiled and stuck out her hand. "Welcome to our town and I hope it is more than you ever dreamed." She left him to drink his beer so she could get ready for her regulars.

Dee had the register set up when the front door opened. In walked Headphone Harry. Headphone Harry rode around town on his bicycle and *always* had his headphones on. Never had anyone seen him without them.

Rumor had it that back in the seventies, a song he'd written had hit the top of the music charts. Some said that song was what played over and over in his headphones. Dee just believed it was his "happy place." So why should people talk?

Seeing Harry helped Dee realize another fact—she loved her happy place. In her garden, with all the people that she'd loved and lost. *Crazy I may be, but it is my happy place.* Dee turned from the register.

"Hi Harry, want a glass of wine today?"

He always stood at the bar across from the register, because that was the only place where he couldn't see his reflection in the mirrors. At least Dee suspected that was why he stuck to that specific spot.

"Yes, a glass of wine, would be superb," he answered. He had a classy way of speaking, almost as though he was still rich and famous. Dee supposed he still was, or at least he was in his *happy place.*

Time flew by as customers came in and out. The Texan stayed until the after-work crowd started to come in, and then he decided to mosey on home.

New faces filled the bar, making Dee wonder if she and Lizzy should be doing more to keep the new business. This time of the year was when a lot of strangers came into town because it was the start of race week when all sorts of racing fans flocked through town. The next town south of theirs held one of the largest NASCAR races in the country. And, although their town appeared small, they usually got a lot of the over flow of people. Dee jotted down on a piece of paper: *Talk to Lizzy about a bike week BBQ idea.*

*Today was a good day. The smell of spring is definitely peeking its head out, and winter is almost over.* Dee smiled to her reflection in the mirror.

BUCKETS was surely glowing with positive energy. Many hours passed, songs fought their way out of the jukebox to each person they were meant for. Cold beverages delighted the taste buds of all that entered. Before Dee knew it, Lizzy was coming through the door and making her way behind the bar.

She hung her purse on the hook and smiled to Dee who smiled back. "You look good Dee, whole. Did you learn more about your family?" Lizzy cocked her head. "Well, did you?"

"I guess, I might have. I've been reading more entries from my mother's journal. You know, learning at my own pace. Taking my time with all of it. Working things out in my head. Today I had an epiphany, I guess." Dee grinned. "You know why I always loved that old house? You know, the one with the women that owned the tavern?" Dee asked, waiting for a response.

"Of course, that's why we are *here*...BUCKETS was inspired by that story—and that house, I guess." Lizzy looked as puzzled.

"That was *my* great-aunt who owned it." Dee said out loud for the first time in months. "As a matter of fact, I was named after her."

Lizzy's eyes opened wide and her smile spread from ear to ear. "Now *that* is really priceless." Like a child enchanted by a fairytale, Lizzy grabbed Dee's hands. "Tell me more!"

"I know, right?" Dee said "It's like history repeating itself. And she raised my dad after his parents died," Dee whispered so the customers wouldn't over hear what she was saying.

She and Lizzy shared a secret magical world that no one was a part of, or at least that's how she believed. Even if Lizzy didn't believe as strongly about that stuff as she did, what she *did* know is that Lizzy believed in *her*, and that was all that mattered.

"You seem to be finding out more from that chest than we did on the World Wide Web. See? It's not so scary any more, is it?" Lizzy asked then looked around.

"I get this sensation that everything is going to turn out just the way it should, Dee." She inhaled and said, "Joe and I really want to get pregnant. No more contraception." She smiled, her peace obvious.

"I knew that!" Dee said, grabbing Lizzy's shoulders and staring her in the eyes. "This is a big step. It's what you want, isn't it? You seem to be wishy washy about it all."

"Yes. Yes, I thought about it for months now. I want to have a baby! There, I said it out loud!" Lizzy sang out. They wrapped their arms around each other and excitedly hugged.

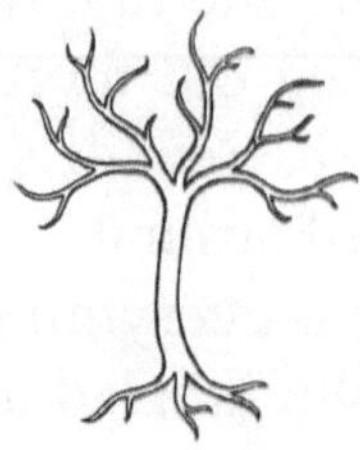

# CHAPTER TWENTY-SIX
## Bonnie and Clyde

*It is in adventure that some people succeed in knowing themselves-in finding themselves.* **Andre Gide**

Bike week approached and motorcycles roared the roads and the tailpipes sang a sweet song of romance. At least Dee felt the romance of it.

Dee loved the idea of holding a man that had the looks of danger and mischief. Bonnie and Clyde was her idea of a romantic couple.

Secretly she desired to have a man hold her and make her feel loved, which was something she had never gotten from her father.

It had been quite a while since she had been with a man. Before she discovered who he really was and that he had a wife and family he'd failed to mention, Leroy always helped fulfill her yearnings for sex. Now, she'd lost the desire, but something about the roar of those cycles had her hormones racing. The need was back and it had roared into town with those motorcycles. She didn't want a relationship necessarily, just a one-night or maybe two, depending on how sexy he was.

She was day dreaming as a group of bikers zoomed past her on the road. She was on her way to open BUCKETS and start preparing for the big Bike Week B-B-Q she and Lizzy had planned for tomorrow. One hundred pounds of smoked Boston butt, baked beans and cole slaw.

Springtime never seemed to last but a few weeks. It always seem like winter would end and summer weather began. If you didn't stop and take notice you would miss that spring had even happened.

Dee pulled into the parking lot of BUCKETS. She noticed Lizzy's Jeep was already there. Lizzy mentioned getting the smoker going early to make sure the meat was good and tender for tomorrow. And, considering the fact that it was one hundred pounds, the meat was going to take a long time to cook. Even so, Lizzy was almost too early to be getting started.

Dee made her way to the door and unlocked it to see Lizzy sitting at the bar looking sad. Her face was in her hands.

"Hey there," Dee said as she walked through the door and made her way to Lizzy. "Are you okay?" Dee noticed Lizzy hadn't reacted to her greeting.

"I got my period today." Lizzy exhaled into her hands and never looked up. "I *so* thought I was pregnant and I'm not."

"Hey...Look at me," Dee said, lifting Lizzy's chin out of her hands. "When it is your time it will happen. Don't try to force your fate. You'll see."

"I know...Just *really* thought I was. I guess, I hoped for it so much, I convinced myself I was."

"We have a big week ahead of us and I couldn't have you getting all morning sick on me, now could I?" Dee smiled.

"I know. You're right." Lizzy stood.

"Besides I need to get some help trained around here first. Gracey and I won't be able to take care of this place without some help," Dee said.

"Oh gosh Dee... I never even thought about that." Lizzy's red-rimmed eyes filled with tears again. "I will work as long as I'm able. I do want to have time off, after the baby is born. Who's going to do all the cooking and soup specials?" Lizzy babbled her way to the kitchen.

"Oh boy, that girl can worry," Dee whispered as she made her way behind the register to set it up for business.

"You are right. I need to get to work on making sure stuff is taken care of here, before I get upset for not being pregnant," Lizzy yelled out through the kitchen doorway.

Dee snickered, shaking her head. *She's been a bit obsessed with the whole baby thing.*

The next day, BUCKETS was filled with locals and many new faces from all over the country. The Bike Week event had become so successful that locals took their vacations the week it was going on, just to enjoy all the festivities. Most of the bars in the area worked together on their scheduled B-B-Q's, to insure that the bikers had a meal every night of the event.

Dee and Lizzy noticed that many of the bikers weren't actually bikers. They were doctors and lawyers that would grow their beards out for that week and live the biker life style. Although, there were the hardcore bikers that were members of various clubs that butted heads. They were easy to spot as they had distinctive logos and club crests that identified them by group. They called it wearing their colors.

Because of complaints and problems south of town with the clubs, Dee and Lizzy posted signs to keep the peace with the biker patrons. *Colors* were forbidden in BUCKETS.

The sign, said "No Colors Allowed!" Unfortunately, because it had to very large, it could be read from the main street that passed the plaza.

Some of the black folks that lived in town took it to mean "no coloreds." When the girls heard that they were shocked because neither one of them harbored any racist beliefs at all.

If anything, Dee held great respect for black people and the things they'd endured. She blamed the misunderstanding on the fact that their county had been one of the last to desegregate their schools, and that only happened a few years before Dee was born.

"Why are people so against one another? I can't comprehend it. They just look for people to not like them, instead of coming together." Dee gritted her teeth as they hustled plates of B-B-Q and buckets of beer to the customers, still thinking of a conflict two men had gotten into earlier. The more people around, the more likely a conflict would manifest.

"Just seems to be there is good and bad everywhere. They assume everyone is against them I guess, but not us, right Dee?" Lizzy smiled as she passed a bucket of beer over top of the bar to a bad boy biker that Dee had been giving gracious glances at.

He seemed to be liked by all of the people that he conversed with. Dee took notice that no ring or ring-shaped tan line danced along his fingers. He was sexy and he rode a motorcycle to boot. His black silky hair was long and neatly pulled back into a pony tail. Gorgeous tattoos ran up his olive complexioned arms.

He had a tenderness about the way he spoke and his smile was the best part yet. He could be her Clyde, and she could be his Bonnie, at least for the week.

"Hey, Miss. Do you ride?" he asked Dee. She realized her glance had turned into a stare.

"I love motorcycles and riding, yes I do," Dee stuttered. Then she smiled.

"Wanna take a ride with me later? You know, once you get off from work. I'm a nice guy, I promise." He smiled, took a sip of his beer and never took his eyes off of her. "I would love to take a beautiful adventure with you. My bike *loves* red heads."

*Um um. I need some of that.* She tried not to look desperate. "Yeah, maybe," she replied. "Let me check with Lizzy, she's the boss." She turned away from him.

She gave Lizzy wide-eyed look, one that only Lizzy would understand. They had their own language and it often didn't require words. Dee saw Lizzy's agreement. *He sure is gorgeous and wants to give me a ride.*

"Lizzy would you mind closing up for me tonight? I got an offer to go for a ride," Dee yelled.

"No problem," Lizzy answered, then smiled.

Dee knew what Lizzy was thinking and she was probably even giggling on the inside. It might not lead to sex, but it was surely what she was needing at the moment. A good looking man to sit close to and wrap her arms around with the humming of a motor between her legs.

*Bonnie and Clyde.*

## CHAPTER TWENTY-SEVEN
### Free Spirit

*I am not an adventurer by choice but by fate."* **Vincent Van Gogh**

Hours later, Gracey showed to help with the night crowd. Lizzy nodded to Dee.

Dee had thoughts of running home to freshen up because her bad-boy biker was not back yet. She threw her back pack over her shoulder and headed out the door of BUCKETS straight to her truck. There he was, leaning on his motorcycle that was just as beautiful and wild as he was. *Tight faded jeans, biker boots, sleeveless black leather vest and arms that screamed to embrace her.*

The bike was sleek and black, mostly built for the driver, but she noticed the long, chromed pull-back bars that would allow him to rest back between her legs. She almost panted thinking about it.

"Hey... ready for that ride?" he asked with a slight tilt of the head.

More than you know, she thought.

"Oh sure." She tucked her keys in her pocket and slung the back pack over both shoulders. He handed her a helmet.

"I had to go borrow a helmet for you. That's where I took off to." He stood in front of her and helped her strap the helmet on. Then he lifted her chin. "You have such beautiful green eyes."

"Thanks," Dee wasn't one to get embarrassed and blush. Especially not for a man, but this one made her blush. Although she was about to jump on the back of a bike with a stranger, she decided not to ask him his name. She needed-that was all. No strings attached or names. She liked the mystery of it, all of it. Two strangers being who-ever they wanted—or needed—to be.

They both saddled up onto the bike and purred out of BUCKETS parking lot. They rode for miles on long, straight roads. He told her to grab the bars and drive when he leaned forward, so when he leaned low over the tank, she did. And loved it. *Bonnie and Clyde.*

*Now this is living.* All the excitement made Dee want to do something outrageous. Her adrenaline was flowing like liquid through her veins. Veins she thought might never feel again, but there it was, her blood pumping like mad.

"Let's stop at that biker bar at the edge of town," he yelled over top of the roar of the motorcycle and piercing wind.

"Sure, I could use a beer," she yelled back.

Wind blowing, motor roaring, and the hum of the bike between her legs made him even sexier than she first thought. They pulled into the bar at the edge of town, which was known to all the local bikers, it was their stomping grounds. The place was packed. Even the picnic tables and benches scattered out front of the building were filled with bikers and black leather.

Dee slowly swung her leg over the fender of the bike and started to remove her helmet. *Man do I feel hot and bad to the bone.* She removed her helmet and with both hands, fluffed her hair.

She swayed her head a few times to undo the damage done by the hot helmet. Her red hair flowed back and forth as she stood beside the sexy stranger. *I'm living and on the wild side.* She fought back a giggle.

"Come on, let's get a drink," he nudged.

"Sounds like a plan." Dee followed with shoulders back, head high, and added that tough biker woman look to her face. *So sexy he was.* She watched him from behind in his faded jeans and leather.

They approached the bar. He ordered them a round of beers and two shots. Dee smiled when he insisted on paying. They slammed the shot and slugged their beers simultaneously and smiled at each other.

"I needed this!" she said over top of the live band that played on the stage. He leaned in so close she could smell the sweet beer lingering on his breath, only inches from her mouth.

"I can give you anything you need," he whispered, at least that was what Dee thought—or hoped—she heard.

Dee really didn't want a relationship and definitely didn't want to fall in love again. She just wanted *sex. No strings, no broken heart and no one to worry about dying on me. I can pretend I'm not who I am for one evening-or two.*

"Let's do another shot!" she yelled above the music.

"You got it!"

He turned to the bartender and yelled. Then he turned to Dee and smiled. She almost could hear his thoughts and it was exactly what she wanted to hear. He too seemed to want a night or two as well. That thought comforted her.

Several beers and shots later, they stumbled their way out of the bar and back to the bike. Dee sat down side saddle and smiled profusely. "I want you! I need you bad!" Then followed with a smile.

"I can and I will help you with that, pretty lady." He leaned in and gently pressed his soft moist mouth to hers. The cold leather from the vest he wore was melting over top of her like wax dipping from a candle.

"Not here... let's get a room," she whispered, not actually wanting to stop.

So, maybe that bad-girl image she had of herself *did* still have a few rules to follow.

## CHAPTER TWENTY-EIGHT
### Vanished

*We all know, from what we experience with and within ourselves that our conscious acts spring from our desires and our fears. Intuition tells us that is true also of our fellows and of the higher animals. We all try to escape pain and death, while we seek what is pleasant...* **Albert Einstein**

They pulled into a hotel south of town that sat beside the interstate. She glanced across the street and noticed the gas station she had called Lizzy from the day she'd had her "flat tire." She chuckled to herself. *Never thought I be here only months later.*

They got a room and Dee insisted on paying. From Dee's perspective, he didn't seem willing to fight over it. They made their way to the room and he stopped her. "By the way, what's your name?" he asked.

"Deidra," she answered.

"I'm..." He started to introduce himself and Dee quickly put her finger to his lips to stop him.

"I have no need for your name," she whispered and that excited her more. The mystery of their rendezvous was what she needed and that was all.

They entered the room that smelled of disinfectant and fresh clean sheets. Dee made her way to the lamp that stood at the bedside table, turned it on. Over top of the bed was a painting of an apple tree that almost looked like a human figure, complete with arms, handing out an apple with one of its limbs.

Dee turned and the handsome biker stood in the glow of the light. She smiled. He unbuttoned his vest one button at a time as Dee made her way to him slowly. She helped remove it from his broad shoulders. Not only did the beautiful art work dance across his body, but under it all was a perfect male physique. *Almost a sculpture of perfection.* Dee ran her hand down his bare chest admiring every toned curve. *I need this.*

She undressed, never once taking her eyes off of him. He seemed as mesmerized by her flawless body as she was to his. They embraced and their roaming hands moved with near desperation to feel every part of each other's perfection.

They used their lips and mouths to caress one another, as if to taste each other's thoughts or to mask words that didn't need to be said. He lowered Dee onto the bed as if she was a delicate, porcelain doll that would break if handled too roughly. Dee indulged in the fruits of love, without the concern of a painful ending.

Many hours later she woke and lay quietly breathing, hoping not to wake the not-so-bad biker who was gently breathing his sweet breath to her ear.

*Why did I need this so much?* It wasn't the sex, though that had been terrific. It was the embrace and love of a man, which she had so desperately needed, even if it was only for the night. So far, none of the men she'd loved had been allowed to stay with her, their lives temporary at best. Obviously, that was her destiny, to find love where she could, always understanding it would not be hers for long.

But last night was what she had needed and there she didn't have an inch of guilt or regret.

Then she thought back to her childhood. Her mother had never felt the love of a man as long as Dee could remember. *My mother had to have had the yearning as well as I, but she fatefully waited for my father's return. Maybe that is why I am the way that I am. I don't want to get hurt again.*

Dee slowly slid out from under his beautifully sculptured arms and quickly dressed. She quietly slipped out the door so he would not awaken.

The sun looked as though it had just risen, glowing bright and shiny. She crossed over the road and made her way to the pay phone. She dropped a quarter and a dime into the slot and dialed.

"Hey Ripley, It's me, Dee. Do you think you could come pick me up? I need a ride," she said. Then she listened.

"No, Lizzy wouldn't understand," Dee confessed. She smiled as Ripley replied.

"Thank you. It means a lot. I'll explain when you get here. I'm at the gas station by the interstate."

"Yeah, that one. Okay, bye." Dee hung up the phone receiver.

About twenty minutes later, Ripley pulled in with one of the hardware store trucks. Ripley had actually been preparing for a delivery when Dee called which worked out perfectly.

Dee jumped into the front seat and smiled at her friend.

"You've been up to no good, I know." Ripley shook her pointer finger at Dee and her eyes squinted and a smirk on her face.

"Yep, and I have no regrets either, just get me the hell out of here before I fall in love again." Dee laughed.

Dee sighed contentedly. Ripley had been Dee's first roommate and had always understood her wild side a little better than Lizzy. Lizzy didn't get it but she accepted it. Eventually Dee would tell her, but right now she wasn't ready to explain.

"You want me to run you to your house?" Ripley asked.

"No, take me by BUCKETS to get my truck. Lizzy won't be there for another hour or so. I hope..." Dee babbled as she stared out the window then turned to Ripley and smiled.

"Guess you can fill me in on the details of your adventure later, then. Over dinner one night?" Ripley hinted.

"You know it." Dee smiled again and then turned her gaze out the window as flashes of light and trees raced past her eyes. But the sunshine stayed as still as her heart.

## CHAPTER TWENTY-NINE
### Confessions

*Whoever confesses and renounces, finds mercy.*
**Proverbs 28:13**

Hours later, after retrieving her truck from BUCKETS, Dee tended her garden. She moved about singing a song of hope as she picked weeds from the flower beds. She noticed the awful cockle plant was not gone, but it was manageable.

"Just one good scoop and to the fire pit you go," she said aloud as she used the hand shovel to dig into its root. *Gosh, I really have to tell Lizzy about last night. She'll hate me if I don't or at least think I'm keeping things from her. And that's not good.* Dee dreaded it, but knew it was the right thing to do. *She always accepts me and my way of thinking. Why am I so worried?*

"Work is done out here," she said as she wiped her hands on her pants. She passed the garden and headed for the front door. She noticed Johnny outside of the garage talking to Beth. They looked like a happy couple. Dee really liked Beth, she was good for Johnny.

"Hey guys, beautiful day today," Dee yelled across the street.

"Sure is!" Johnny hollered.

"Hello Dee! Nice to see you, it's been a while!" Beth followed.

"We need to get together some time," Dee called back as she opened the screen door.

She entered the house, stopped in the middle of the living room floor. *What should I do first? Call Lizzy? The chest? The journal maybe? Or the Web search for my father?*

She thought a moment. *One thing at a time, Dee.* She decided the most important deed needed to be done first.

"Lizzy it is," Dee announced as she made her way to the phone. She dialed the number.

"BUCKETS, how can I help you?" Came through the line and it wasn't Lizzy.

"Gracey? What are you doing there?" Dee asked.

"Lizzy needed to go to the doctor this morning. I guess it was kind of last minute."

"Is everything okay?" Dee asked, battling the panic in her chest.

"Oh yeah, it's just some kind of checkup. You know Lizzy, she thinks because she hasn't gotten pregnant that something is wrong with *her*. I think she just wanted insight. You know, to make sure her and Joe are doing it *right.*" Gracey giggled.

"Thank God that's all it is." Dee exhaled. "Okay...Are you working all day?"

"Yeah, at least that's what I am assuming."

"All right see you at six then. I'll try giving her a call at the house," Dee said.

She hung up the phone and thought again about Lizzy's car phone idea. *I really need to get this dreaded conversation over with.*

"Okay chest, looks like *you* are next!" she said, staring at the chest on the floor where it waited patiently since the day she brought it in from the truck. Yep, been sitting there for a while not being ignored. Whatever it was, it had to happen now. *Timing is everything.*

Dee sat Indian style on the floor in front of the chest. She slowly opened it. There were two ceramic Indian pieces that she took out one by one. They looked as though they were hand painted. One statue was an Indian chief with a head dress on. The other, a beautiful Indian women sitting side saddle on a horse wearing a tan dress, with turquoise wraps in her hair.

*I wonder if these represent my mother and father?* Dee admired the ceramic pieces. She placed them off to the side. She pulled a dream catcher from the chest. The dream catcher looked handmade. She stood, then strolled to her room as she admired it.

Above her bed was a nail that once held the picture of her mother that now sat on top of her computer desk. She hung the dream catcher, climbed down off the bed and stepped back to admire it.

She made her way back to the chest and flopped back down on the floor in front of it. As she looked in the chest again, there was a knock at the door.

"Come in!" she yelled, not budging from the floor.

"Hi!" Lizzy poked her head in. "I was hoping you were home," she said as she let herself in.

"I'm here. How was the doctor's visit?" Dee asked.

"Fine, healthy as a horse the doctor says." Lizzy said as she too flopped down onto the floor in front of the chest. "Is this the first time you looked in it since that first night months ago?"

"Yep!" Dee said with a tight-lipped smile, then decided to speak. "I am amazed at how much I never knew about my parents. I feel slightly betrayed, as if they were keeping a lifetime of secrets from me." Dee stared for a minute and realized she too had been keeping secrets from Lizzy. It may have been only a few hours but she now understood.

"Lizzy, I had a one-nighter last night. I know you don't understand it or approve. I don't expect you to, either. I just needed to tell you so you didn't think I was keeping things from you. You know, secrets."

Lizzy smiled. "I have to confess something myself... Joe and I have been trying to have a baby for quite a while now. I was afraid you wouldn't agree with my decision. Before we even went away on the trip to the expo and the witch's town. I'm sorry I didn't tell you sooner." Lizzy slung her arm over Dee's shoulder and rubbed her knuckles across the top of Dee's head. "Was he any good?" She giggled.

Dee grinned like a cat that had caught a mouse. "I would say, the best I've had in a while." Dee shrugged.

"Is that why you went to the doctor? Because you aren't pregnant yet?" Dee asked.

"Yep I'm starting to think something is wrong with me, down there." Lizzy chuckled out. "He said I'm fine and I am probably trying too hard."

"Okay, then. Let's see what other treasures are in this chest," Dee said, changing the subject. *Things sure are easier to go through with Lizzy around. So why not finally get this chest over with once and for all?*

They pulled out some old photos that lay on the bottom. One was the one Dee remembered from the first night, the picture of the old house and the two women and little boy on the porch. Now the picture did not scare her because she knew it wasn't the angry boy she kept seeing on her dresser, it was her father at a young age. The others were various pictures of the old house.

Then there it was, a picture of her mother and father. They stood side by side on what appeared to be the Indian reservation. They were dressed in Indian attire and holding hands.

"This must be their wedding picture." Dee turned her head to Lizzy. "They were spiritually married by the shaman of the tribe. I read about this in my mother's journal."

"How cool is that." Like a child at the feet of a favorite storyteller, Lizzy snuggled closer to get a look at the picture.

Dee smiled at her and was truly grateful she had Lizzy in her life. She also had great appreciation for Lizzy because she had saved her life.

*What a beautiful life I have.*

## CHAPTER THIRTY
### Obsessions

*In nature, nothing is perfect and everything is perfect. Trees can be contorted, bent in weird ways, and they are still beautiful. Alice Walker*

After Bike Week, the out-of-towner's slowly made their way back to the places they had come from.

Dee and Lizzy's work week's fell back into the normal routine. Business continued to grow as new people came into the area to live or work. Lizzy became less obsessed with getting pregnant and started "spring cleaning" as she called it.

Everything was getting organized. The spices in the kitchen, the cutlery, even the beer and wines were in alphabetical order. Dee was afraid to stand in one place for long.

"I just straightened up all of these wine bottles yesterday. How come they are all mixed up again?" Lizzy asked Dee.

"Don't know," Dee said with a smirk. "Maybe Gracey and I were looking for a certain kind. We might have just moved them around a bit. Maybe you should alphabetize them, to make it easier for us." Dee smirked again as she grabbed a piece of ice to chew on.

The phone rang and Lizzy picked up the receiver.

"BUCKETS. May I help you?" She listened, her brows pulled together in a frown.

"Who? No...No one works here by that name. I told you that the last time you called." Lizzy glanced at Dee and shrugged her shoulders.

"I'm sorry. Glad you understand. Good bye." Lizzy hung up the phone and turned to Dee.

"That's strange... I keep getting these phone calls, a man asking if a Deidra works here," Lizzy said to Dee.

Dee eyes widened before she could catch herself.

"Oh my gosh Dee, is that him? You know, the one nighter?"

"Good chance it was. Lizzy, I don't want him to know who I am, so you haven't lied," Dee explained, knowing Ms. Lizzy Righteous wouldn't willingly tell a lie.

"I don't think you'll have to worry about him calling any more. He sounded upset but said he understood where I stood."

Silence dangled in the air for a moment and it wasn't their usual comfortable silence. Dee made her way back over to the wine bottles and rearranged them in front of Lizzy and snickered.

"I knew it was you doing this shit on purpose. I knew it." Lizzy laughed. "I honestly thought I was taking the organizing crap a little too personal any way."

"Wow, Ms. Righteous, you got the mouth of a trucker." Dee smiled popping another ice cube in her mouth. "Are you and Joe gonna go to the county fair next weekend?"

"Yeah, Both of Lynn's boys are showing their pigs for the Future Farmers of America. Did you know the local feed store donated feed for the boys and other kids too?" Lizzy answered as she straightened the wine bottles again. "We'll probably go Saturday night," she added as the last bottle was straightened.

"Maybe I'll meet you there. We got Gracey helping to train the new girl that night. So...yeah, maybe I'll go too."

Dee walked to the end of the bar and picked up a local newspaper. "Look, coupons too."

"You know we got a lot of the carnie folks last year," Lizzy said.

Dee nodded. Some of the regular customers called the fair workers "carnie crew." They shared strange stories of their life on the road. Most of them were good people, they were just different. A lot of them were loners and it was just who they were. They traveled the country setting up from county to county, all over the United States. They never stayed at a single area more than a week. Their homes were tents and campers, nothing stable or permanent.

"It is sad that BUCKETS is their only life when they are here," Dee mumbled as she looked at the newspaper.

Lizzy shrugged. "Well, they work long hours when they're in town, too. They're probably too tired to do much else. I'm glad they come here, though."

Once again, St. Patrick's Day came around and one of their favorite customer's, Manny, made an annual visit for Lizzy's corned beef and cabbage dinner. Manny and his wife had been the first couple to sit at the bar when BUCKET'S opened, and just before his wife passed away from cancer, Manny had delivered her recipe to Lizzy. As a tribute to friendship and tradition, Lizzy prepared the meal with extra love for their customers.

"Did you turn on the OPEN sign, Dee?" Lizzy asked as she set up the register.

"Not yet, I'll get it." Dee put the paper down and made her way to the sign and pulled the cord. In walked a customer.

"Oh yeah, Lizzy, Manny was in after you left yesterday. He finished off the last of the corned beef and cabbage," Dee announced so Lizzy didn't try to promote the special they no longer had.

"Wow, smells nice and clean in here," the customer said as he made himself at home at the bar.

"Yeah, Mrs. Clean—Mr. Clean's wife—is going to be your hostess for the duration," Dee blurted with a smile. Lizzy snarled at Dee, then turned to the customer and smiled.

"What can I get you to drink?"

"Ice cold mug of draft beer," he said. "How about some hot wings?"

"You got it! I guess I'll need to *clean* off the SPECIALS board..." Lizzy babbled to herself. "Wings it is."

Lizzy went to work. First, the frosted mug of beer, then headed to the kitchen for the wings.

Dee poked her head into the kitchen. "See you at six. I gotta go get some laundry done. My house chores are piling up on me." Dee smiled. "I promise whatever you organize tonight I won't touch. Okay?"

Lizzy busily worked in the kitchen, then stopped and wrinkled her nose. "I guess I went a little overboard. I will say this, it has been keeping my mind off of not getting pregnant." She smiled again, then started working again. She dropped a dozen wings into the hot sizzling oil.

Dee strolled past the gentleman who sipped on his frosty mug absorbing the news on the TV.

She walked into the beautiful spring sunshine with the crisp breeze that joined it and watched as the cedar trees across the way swayed as if bowing to the breeze.

*Today is a good day. Thank you, God, for this beautiful day.*

## CHAPTER THIRTY-ONE
## Daisy Field

*Solitary trees, if they grow at all, grow strong* **Winston Churchill**

Dee sat out on the swing in the garden admiring the bright yellow-green sprouts of all the seedlings that were pushing their way up through the soil. This year was going to be a year of abundant growth for her garden. It was already starting to flourish and spring had just begun.

"I probably need to go see what Johnny is up to. He hasn't pulled any pranks lately," Dee said to a bumble bee that kept buzzing around her head.

If she didn't know better she would have thought the bee was trying to tell her something. She made her way across the street. Johnny lay on the ground under a suped-up mud truck.

"Hey Johnny! How's business?" Dee cocked her head to get a view of what he was working on.

"Howdy, Dee, Do you like my butterfly?" Johnny asked as he turned the wrench below.

"Very cool. This is your new adventure?"

"Yup, getting her ready for the ten-thousand dollar mud bog event old Danny Johnston is having this week end. I love me some muddin'," Johnny drawled as he finished tightening nuts.

He slid out and away, then sat up on his creeper. "Can ya hand me that shop rag, Dee? And don't touch none of my shit-ya hear?" He chuckled.

Dee smiled. *He knows me too well.* She tossed him the rag.

"What you gonna name her?" Dee asked.

Johnny always named his vehicles after a woman. Dee always wondered how he came up with some of the names he had. His tractor's name was Old Betsy, and his other truck was Wanda. *This one is bound to be a good name, too.*

"Winnnn-Dee, get it?" He laughed and got to his feet. He paced around the truck for a minute.

"Maybe I'll come up and watch ya this weekend..." Dee said as she started browsing through the tool box. *I'm not going to mess with him today—it will be more fun watching him squirm thinking I did.*

"Ya know Dee, I've been doing a lot of thinking about our talk way back. You know, about chasing butterflies? I can honestly say if it wasn't for you and Lizzy, I'd still be at my daddy's farm waiting for something to happen for me. You girls showed me to go after the things I want." He struggled to get out the next words. "So, I thank you, and love you girls to pieces. And I do not mean that in a boyfriend, girlfriend way either."

"Awww. That's so sweet Johnny! I think that the people that come into our lives, even if it's for a brief time, are there to give us our perfect plan." Dee gave him an extra wide grin and winked at him. *That will make him even more nervous.*

Johnny wiped his forehead with the greasy shop rag which put a giant strip of grease across his forehead and made it look as though he had a uni-brow. At that moment a customer pulled in to the parking area and Johnny turned to greet them.

"Johnny!" Dee gasped. *This could be a good prank but I'd rather see him worry.* She pointed to his forehead. "You got some grease there."

Johnny wiped his face clean, gave her grin, and then went out to take care of his customer.

Dee made her way back across the street. She returned to her swing and noticed the cockle plant had not returned.

*Maybe I finally got rid of that weed once and for all.* As she swung in the swing she drifted off to sleep...

*Dee was walking through dense fog, a place that felt familiar. With each step, the fog moved away from her feet, as though to show her the way.*

*She noticed trees of all shapes and sizes standing tall and proud. Dee could tell from her instincts that it wasn't a scary place at all. It was a lonely and cumbersome place. The more steps she took the more the fog shifted away.*

*She noticed two small bare feet peeking out from the other side of a willow tree at the edge of the mystical forest she was exploring.*

*She moved toward them to find the angry boy sitting at the base with his arms still folded, and still pouting like a child that was not getting his way.*

*Dee knelt down. "Hi, what's your name?"*

*"I don't know," he replied.*

*"Why are you so upset and sad?" she asked.*

*"My mommy said I have to stay here until she is ready. Then I can get to run through the daisy field, and play, but not until she is ready. It's not fair," the boy huffed.*

*"I am sure your mommy has good intentions," Dee offered, trying to console him.*

*"She is afraid I might get hurt, or lost, or something..." he continued.*

*"I'm sure she just loves you a whole bunch, and wants you safe. My father left me as a young girl...to keep me safe. It made*

*me sad too, but now I understand why, and someday you will understand, too."*

*"How will I ever know what the daisy field looks like, or how fun it is if I'm stuck here?" he asked.*

"Dee? Are you awake?" a voice asked. Dee opened her eyes and a dark silhouette blocked the sun from shining onto her face. It was Ripley.

"Yeah, yeah." She sat up from the swing.

"I was dropping off your sweat shirt. You must have left it in the truck that day I picked you up," Ripley said as she tossed the sweat shirt to Dee.

"Cool. Thanks again for the ride," Dee said with a smile.

"Did you ever get a chance to explain to Lizzy?" Ripley asked.

"I did, I did. She took it well, always does."

"So, tell me all the juicy goodness," Ripley said, curling her nose and rubbing her hands to together like a child expecting candy from a candy store.

"He was beautiful, Rip! He was a bad boy biker, just how I like em. Sexy, oh so sexy." Dee's eyes rolled back into her head. She took a whiff of the sweat shirt hoping to smell his scent, but it was long gone. "He touched me all over my body, like I was a piece of china that was worthy of worship. It was so great, Rip."

"What was his name?" Ripley asked.

"Don't know, don't care to know either."

"What? Are you kidding me? You can't tell me you aren't the least bit interested?" Ripley gasped.

"Nope, it's better to have felt the joy and know that no pain will come from it. Right?" Dee said as her foot stopped the swing. She looked at Ripley and waited for her answer.

"I don't know, Dee. You've had a lot of losses and a lot of pain, so I'm sure not going to tell you you're wrong. I'm not sure it would work for me, though." Ripley stood.

"I've got to get back to work. Lindsey is starting to play tee-ball this year, so we have to go get a mitt for her to play. The hardware store is sponsoring her team, so I'm also responsible for the uniforms. Ahhh...welcome to my crazy life."

As they walked toward Ripley's truck, she stopped and put her hand on Dee's arm. "I think you were doing the right thing just having the one nighter. Ripley smiled as she hopped in the truck. "I think... I might have a little tingle of jealousy right now."

## CHAPTER THIRTY-TWO
### County Fair

***Joy is a net of love by which you can catch souls.*Mother Teresa**

Saturday came and Dee planned to meet Lizzy and Joe after work to go to the County Fair. Dee stood at the register with her back to the bar counting out the day-shift receipts.

"Hello, beautiful!" a man's voice rang out above the chatter of the after-work crowd.

Dee hesitated, then slowly turned to see the face she had dreaded seeing for months now. There he was standing at the bar with a smile on his face.

"Well, imagine seeing you here," she said. "Been busy truckin', I suppose."

*I can't believe he has the nerve to show his face here. Although he has no clue that I know he is married. Hmmm...Maybe I should play this out?*

"Yeah, been crazy busy, nonstop loads. They took me off of my Florida route, that's why I haven't come by. Making good money, though," Leroy explained.

Dee faked a smile. What she wanted to do was fly across the bar and strangle him, after she told him what she thought of him. She held back and spoke with grace.

"Wanna beer?" she asked as she tossed a coaster onto the bar.

"Sure." Leroy dug in his pocket and pulled out a fifty dollar bill and slid it across the bar and whispered, "And you."

Dee grabbed the fifty then handed it back and said, "I've got this one." She knew she needed to do something and do something now before he tried to go any further.

"Leroy, I forgive you." Dee smiled then continued, "I hope your wife and children do the same. Whatever has happened is between you and God. He too, is forgiving."

"What happened to you Dee? You gone all religious on me?" Leroy asked. "And how did you know I was married?"

"I called and spoke to your wife."

Leroy's face turned white as a ghost. "She knows?" Leroy's voice went a pitch or two higher.

"You were gone so long, I called to check on you and she answered the phone. I didn't want to cause her pain, so I didn't tell her anything. I told her I was taking a survey. She knows she deserves a faithful man who does not stray, though."

"Damn it, Dee!" he said. Some of his color had come back, but his eyes were sad.

"I've learned to love myself, and as for you..." Dee walked out from behind the bar and stood in front of him. "You should too," she whispered and gave him a pat on the cheek.

"Now, get on outta here!" she yelled, pointing to the door.

Leroy made his way to the door, glanced back at Dee then hung his head as he exited BUCKETS.

*Wow that felt good! I have to say that was the dark cave I thought I was going to get sucked into and I overcame it!*

Dee looked up from the cloud of heart-racing adrenaline. Gracey, the new girl Angel, and ten customers all starred at Dee with their mouths opened wide enough to catch a hundred flies. BUCKETS was quiet, but only for a moment.

"You go, girl!"Gracey cried through the silence.

The rest of BUCKETS cheered with applause, as if Dee had just won the Boston marathon. Dee took a bow and finished up her work before Lizzy and Joe arrived.

Moments later, Lizzy walked through the door. Dee could not wait to share her news.

"Guess who showed up here today?" Dee asked Lizzy.

"Oh my gosh, the one nighter?" Lizzy replied wide-eyed and ready to listen.

"No... Leroy!" Dee hissed.

"No freakin' way!" Lizzy said, "You told him how it was. Right?"

Dee grinned. "Sure did and it felt good."

"She sure did,"Gracey confirmed with a smile then went back to work.

"He's lucky I wasn't here. I would have scratched his eyes out!" Lizzy shrieked as she wrapped her arms around Dee. About that time Joe poked his head in the door and waved at them to come.

"I got the car running," he mouthed.

*****

The happy trio entered the gates of the fair and worked their way through the crowd to get a glimpse of Lizzy's nephew's showing their pigs at the auction.

"Wow, Jeremy got a blue ribbon for Wilbur, and Phillip got a blue ribbon for his pig, too," Lizzy announced as she stood on her tip-toes to see over the bidders. She stretched her neck from side to side just to catch a peek.

After that was all said and done they made their way to the food tent. Dee was starving and ordered almost one of everything they sold. They collected their food and sat at a picnic table outside in the picnic grove.

"You really going to eat all of that?" Joe asked. Lizzy giggled as they sat down with their chili dogs and sodas.

"Darn sure gonna try," Dee said through her mouth full of corn dog.

"Dee loves her food," Lizzy remarked. "She has a hard time resisting yummy smellin' food."

Dee ate every bit and by the look on Joes face he was amazed. They then shuffled their way to the rides. That was time for Joe to indulge. The three of them did every ride that had signs for fifty six inches and up.

Dee wasn't so happy with that idea, but only realized why after the fact.

Some of the carnie crew were the same faces as last year's group and they told Dee and Lizzy they would be sure to stop by BUCKETS when they could.

It wasn't long after the last ride that Dee leaned against a power pole and clutched her belly.

"My stomach ain't feeling so good..." Dee moaned. "Are ya'll almost ready to go?" she moaned again. "I don't mean to be a party pooper but I ain't feelin' good."

"It's probably all that food you ate and the rides. Not a good combination, Dee," Joe chuckled.

"Probably your nerves from the Leroy drama," Lizzy added.

"Don't know, I just know I'm about to..." Dee took off running for the restrooms that stood behind the entrance gates.

A few minutes later, she heard Lizzy's voice just outside the stall.

"Dee? Are you alright?"

"I am bad sick, Liz... huaggg!" *I think I just might die…*

"Okay, when you are able, we'll get you back to the house. We'll be outside when you're ready."

She had no idea how long she stayed in that fairgrounds bathroom, but Dee couldn't get back to the house soon enough.

When Lizzy and Joe helped her into the house, she promised them she'd be fine, so they went on home. But Dee ended up sleeping out in the hall right next to the bathroom.

Sure was a good time, though, she thought, even with being sick. She was going to miss the carnival workers if they stopped in tonight that was for sure.

If she got enough rest, maybe tomorrow she could bless them with her presence. She scrambled to her feet and reached the toilet just in time.

*Huagg! Okay, maybe I'll feel well enough tomorrow.*

# CHAPTER THIRTY-THREE
## Unexpected Guest


*Happiness often sneaks through a door you didn't know you left open. John Barrymore*


When Dee woke, noon was long gone and she was still on the floor in the hallway next to the bathroom.

Except for a sour stomach, she felt better. She sat upright and used the wall for support. *Had to be food poisoning.*

She managed to make her way to the kitchen and grabbed some saltines from the cabinet. *Should I call Gracey or Angel to cover for me?*

As the saltine cracker made it way to her stomach it seemed to have eased the sour burn. *Hmmm maybe a few more of these and I won't have to call any one. Tough as nails, I am.*

Dee munched down a few more and realized they were doing the trick. *Few more hours of rest and I'll be back to normal.* Dee made her way to her bed room, lounged across the bed and fell back to sleep.

*She was in the mystical forest moving curiously through the trees. The ground was saturated with wet mud-like material.*

*Each step squished up between her bare toes. She looked behind and around every tree she passed in search of the angry boy.*

*"Where could he be?" She came up on the willow tree where she had first spoke to the angry boy. He was not there either.*

*In the far distance she could hear a young boy calling "Mommy!" The voice seemed to come from the thickest part of the forest. Then another voice rang out from behind her.*

*"Dee!" It was a man's voice. She turned to see who it was. There stood a man holding a little girl's hand. She knew somehow that it was her father, even though she couldn't see his face clearly.*

*The little girl felt familiar too. She forced her eyes to focus and realized it was her younger self. She must have been four or five. She couldn't make out the face of the man, no matter how hard she tried to focus. Her father had left them before she was that age. Her frustration drove her closer.*

*"Mommy?" The young boy's voice rang out again which stopped her in her tracks, but this time it sounded like it was moving closer.*

*She turned in the direction of the voice, then turned back again to try to focus on the face of the man she knew was her father. He was gone.*

*Out of more frustration she spun around to move closer to the young boy's voice and the angry boy stood right in front of her.*

*"Oh!" she gasped, her hand over her pounding heart. "I was looking for you." She knelt to his eye level.*

*"I can't find my mommy," he whimpered....*

Dee felt a sudden jerk as if she'd been sucked from the forest. Then she realized she was awake and anxiety rested heavily in her chest.

She took a glimpse at the clock and realized she only had an hour before she had to be at BUCKETS. She jumped out of bed and rushed to get ready, grabbing some jeans from the dryer.

"Lovely, I am either putting on weight or that dryer heat setting is too high. I'll worry about this later." Dee hopped her way into her jeans all the way down the hall. She'd slept the whole day away, but she felt much better. It was obviously a good use of her time off.

Once she dressed and washed her face, she threw her back pack over her shoulder and went out the door. As she reached for the truck door she stopped, realizing her stomach was still sort of sour feeling so she ran back in to grab the saltines.

"Just in case," she mumbled as she made her way back out to the truck.

She cranked it up, made a quick wave to Johnny who stood outside the garage and headed off to BUCKETS.

Once she arrived she pushed her way through the front door in hopes she made it on time.

"Hey, I was starting to wonder if I was going to work a double tonight," Lizzy said as Dee made her way behind the bar. "How are you feeling?"

"Much better. I think it was a mix of a lot of greasy food and the rides," Dee babbled as she checked out the coolers to see if she needed to stock before tonight's carnie crew came in.

"Dee, you seem a bit distracted lately and then with that episode with Leroy—I'm just concerned about you." Lizzy stopped Dee for a minute to talk. Dee huffed.

"I'm fine, I really am," Dee replied. "Actually, I have felt really good lately, hopeful, and okay with everything. I swear!" Dee stood with her right hand in the air.

"Okay. I'm just concerned." Lizzy turned to grab for her purse. "Do you want me to stay a little while? I could come back and help you close up," she offered.

"I'll be fine!" Dee insisted. "Now go."

Lizzy smiled and made her way to the door still watching Dee. Dee waved Lizzy out the door like she was shooing a pesky fly.

The night seemed to go on forever. At a few points throughout the night it slowed down to only a few customers. After eleven, the carnie crew started arriving one by one. They were hard drinkers. *I understand that. Get as much down time in before moving on to the next city.*

After a few hours they left in the same fashion, one by one. Dee had all her work finished for closing. She clicked the lights off as she made her way to turn off the open sign and lock the door. A man opened the door and staggered in just as Dee went to lock it.

*Must be one of the carnie crew. Good grief, he can hardly walk. I won't serve him but I can't turn him away.*

"I'm sorry, but we are closed," she said, noticing how the smell of whiskey floated around him like a thick fog.

"Ohh, I no need anything," he slurred and pushed his way in. "I quit drinking..."

"Sir, I'm closed," she said to him as he stumbled to the bar.

"I don't drink no more," he slurred as he tried to pull the stool away from the bar.

*Really? I don't need this tonight.* Dee locked the door and made her way behind the bar. *Maybe he will sober up enough to move on.  I have got to finish up here.* Dee stared at him and moved closer. *I know this man from somewhere....*

"I had to come here..." he started again.

"Okay. Just relax a few minutes while I get the bar wiped down but after that buddy, I'm outta here and you can't stay."

Dee wiped the bar and made her way to the register to grab all the receipt's to put them in a folder for Lizzy. She listened to the old man's drunken babble, something about getting to his family to explain. Dee snickered to herself. *He has a lot of explaining to do.*

Once she finished, she walked over to the man. "Hey...time to go." She gently shook him. "Time to go!" she said louder.

Finally after not getting anywhere, she helped him up from the bar stool and out the door. She stood in the parking lot contemplating what she should do with him. Then made her way to her truck, opened the door, and pushed him up into it.

She made her way back to the front door and locked it. She went to her truck and stared again at the drunk man who was now sitting in her passenger seat, passed out. *Lovely.*

She made her way home, pulled into the drive and sat for a moment again and stared at him. *Tonight of all nights.*

She got out, walked around to the passenger side and opened the door. The man's dead weight poured out almost on top of her, but Dee caught him.

She dragged his limp body over to a giant aspen tree that guarded the front corner of her property, and leaned the man up against it. She went to her garden shed, grabbed a piece of rope. She made her way back to the tree, where the drunk man lay. She wrapped the rope around the tree and the man. She tied it as tight as she could, then stood in front of him, staring.

"Now you can't leave, hurt yourself or anyone else for that matter," Dee said to the limp body of the man. She turned, went to her house, opened the door and glanced back one more time before she locked up for the night. *At least he'll be safe.*

She made her way to the kitchen and filled a tall glass of water from the tap and placed it in the refrigerator. *He'll need a cold glass of water when he wakes.*

She made her way to her room, put on her pajamas, and jumped into bed. Moments later she was sound asleep.

## CHAPTER THIRTY-FOUR
### He Shows His Face

**They are wrong who say that love is blind. On the contrary, nothing-not even the smallest detail-escapes the eyes: one sees everything in the loved one, notices everything: but melts it all into one flame with the great and simple: I love you.  Anonymous**

Dee woke before the sun had finished rising. She stood at the front window looking out at the drunk man who was still tied to the tree, as she sipped her herbal tea. She had awakened knowing why he'd seemed familiar.

*I probably should go wake him.* The sunshine was quite bright on his face. She walked to the kitchen, set her coffee cup onto the table and grabbed the glass of cold water from the fridge. She marched outside.

She stood in front of the tree still staring at the man when she heard Johnny yell from across the street

"Dee? Everything alright?"

She saw him looking at the aspen tree and the rope.

"Yep, sure is," she answered back, not wanting to take her eyes off the drunk and still clutching the glass of cold water. She glanced back at Johnny and saw him disappear into his garage, shaking his head.

She knelt down in front of the man, stared some more at him, then threw the cold water into his face. Startled, the drunk man woke, sputtering and shaking the water from his face.

"Hi, Dad!" Dee hissed. Yep, it was her father. She could now see the resemblance to the man in the photo she'd found in the chest. She'd tried for years now to see it in her mind, and here it was tied to *her* tree. "Nice to see you!"

"Dee? Is it really you?" he asked.

"Sure is, Daddy!"

"Thank God, I made it," he said. "I have been trying to get to you. It's really important that I talk with you."

"Really? After all these years you want to talk to me *now*?"

"Dee, there is a curse on our family." He sighed. "We have to do something, we have to find the trunk that holds the curse. I want to free you of the curse. I think I can show you, and together we can break it. We don't have much time," he said as he tried to wiggle his way free of the ropes.

Dee stood. "Sober up old man, then I'll untie you. You'll have to promise you won't leave again."

"That's a deal," he said, his eyes filled with tears.

"Henry Bishop, you finally showed your face..." Dee walked back towards the house. She opened the screen door, entered and let it slam behind her.

She watched for an hour as the beads of sweat rolled down his forehead. She started to feel a sting of sympathy for him, so she made him a peanut butter and jelly sandwich and took it out to him.

She zipped her mouth, scared of saying hateful things that she truly did not mean. She untied the rope and handed him the sandwich.

"Thank you," he said. He held the sandwich and spoke calmly. "Dee, I left to save you, not to ever harm you."

"I know." *So why is he back?*

"We need to find that trunk and stop this curse," he said, still holding the sandwich without taking a bite. *Does that mean he wants to stay with me?*

"I have the Raggedy Ann Chest... There is no curse in it... unless you count the journal of the woman cursed with loving you!" Dee hissed through her teeth.

She took a deep breath. *Okay, let's just go inside and talk like adults.* She untied the rest of the rope and unwrapped it from the tree and spoke again to her father.

"Come on lets go inside—it's cooler in the house." She made her way to the door and he followed. When she was inside, she picked up the phone and dialed.

"Hey Gracey? Could you fill in for me today and tomorrow?" Dee asked.

"Thank you." She paused as if listening. "Yeah, let me talk to her."

She glanced at her father who was sitting on her couch.

"Hey Liz, guess what? I don't need to look for my dad, anymore." Dee smiled at the wall. "Nope, *he* found me." Again she listened for a moment.

"Naw, just a day or two. Oh, he is staying alright. I'm going to make sure of that," Dee said as she glanced at him again. "Thanks, I appreciate it. We gotta lot of catching up to do. All-righty, bye-bye." Dee hung up the phone.

"So, if the chest I have doesn't have this *curse* in it, where might the evil trunk be?"

"I believe it is in my Aunt Deidra's old house somewhere. We need to go and look."

"Well, I just took the next two days off, which should be plenty of time to find some damn curse, maybe fix all these problems of resentment I seem to be having. But first, there are a few things I need to get off my chest." Dee took a very deep breath then spoke.

"You hurt me very bad. You drowned my mother's life with loneliness, and poor Gina never even had a fog of a memory of you."

"Gina? Who is Gina?" he asked.

"Your other daughter. The one my mother was carrying when you left."

"I need to find her," he babbled.

"She's gone. She passed away from a car accident years ago." She watched the color drain out of his face.

"Dee, there are gifts we Bishops have..." he started to say. She stopped him with the lift of her pointer finger.

"I forgive you, and I do love you, but if this relationship is going to work, keep the crazy talk away from my home," she commanded.

"Let's go check out that old house and find this curse that has made everyone's life so miserable. We will settle this once and for all," she growled, holding the door open for him.

Her father stood and went out the front door. At the truck, Dee glanced across the street at Johnny who watched her open the passenger door and close it. She did a quick wave to him and he tilted his cap to her.

*Johnny's probably wondering who the hell this old guy is.* She got in the driver's seat, cranked up the truck and backed out of the drive way.

*I'm wondering that myself.*

## CHAPTER THIRTY-FIVE
## The Curse

*You are my rock and my fortress, for the sake of your name lead and guide me.* **Psalm 31:3**

As Dee drove southwest of town, silence haunted the truck. Dee, not knowing what to say to a father so long gone from her life wondered if she had truly forgiven him. They came upon the old railroad tracks and he finally spoke.

"You see these tracks?" he asked. "As a teenager I got my truck caught over top of these tracks, with my best friend Bubba. Sure thought I was gonna die that day."

He chuckled. "A train was a coming, and we tried everything we could to get her off the tracks. Then we both got to one side and pushed with everything we had. She tumbled over and we fell to the ground seconds before the train came flying by," he said, staring down at the tracks as they crossed.

"It was like an angel or something helped us, pushed us back from harm's way," he said.

Then the old house caught his eye with the giant oak which was even bigger than the last time Dee had been there. The house still slanted sideways and the old bottles still stood at attention in the window boxes on the second floor. The neon signs still hung sadly in the downstairs windows.

Dee and her father sat silently for several moments, then her father spoke.

"I have a lot of childhood memories that still linger here."

That was when Dee realized if she was going to have any relationship with this man, she needed to talk.

"I too have memories of this place," she said as they made their way up the creaking wooden steps. Her father stopped on the porch and looked as though he wanted to hear more.

Dee continued. "I never knew why but this was a secret, special place I would come. I found it not long after I got my driver's license. Momma never knew I knew about this place. I just found it one day. Then, I heard the stories of the women that lived here. I thought it was pointing me to my fate, which is now BUCKETS. That's where you found me. I own that place, I don't just work there," Dee said.

"Then recently, when I found Momma's journal, I found out why the house was important to me. And I learned more about you," she said, now looking into his eyes. *They are very gentle eyes. He really means me no harm.*

She opened the wooden door and waved her hand as if asking him to enter, so he did.

They walked around the first floor in a more comfortable silence. Dee could see his agitation and she understood how anxiety made a person feel. She stayed just a step or two behind him, but they didn't find whatever it was he looked for.

Suddenly he picked up his head and smiled at her. "I got it!" Then he trotted up the staircase and Dee followed.

He stopped at the beginning of the long hallway. Dee suddenly remembered the dream she'd had a few months back. The scene looked exactly the same except that she'd been alone.

He walked all the way to the end of the hall. Dee looked around. There was nothing there.

Then he pointed to the wall. "It's in there," he said.

Dee knelt down in front of the place he indicated. Sure enough, there was a door there. After a couple of minutes, she pried it open and there sat the trunk.

It was bigger than her Raggedy Ann chest, though it looked very similar. She dragged it out from the cubby hole.

"Are you sure the curse is in here?" she asked him.

"Yes," he said as if frightened to get too close to it. "Open it," he whispered.

Dee carefully opened the trunk and looked inside. *I can't believe I am doing this, again.* She noticed that this time she wasn't the one who was scared. Her father was the one who looked as though he feared he might find something that would harm him.

In the trunk were some old jars, with something in them. The contents were sealed by corks. She looked closer.

One held sea salt and the bottle read, *Salt that is pure will protect you from evil.*

The second bottle read, *Sage, this will cleans from negative and wrong doings.*

There were several colored bottles in the trunk. A couple of blue glass ones, a couple of brown and some frosted yellow ones.

*This is odd,* Dee thought as she noticed one had a paper rolled up and sticking out of the top instead of a cork. The paper was obviously old. It felt more like cloth than paper. She slowly unrolled it. Her father watched from over top of her shoulder. The paper read:

*Give to the Bishop that seeks blissful love.*
*Blessed will be given gifts from above.*
*Unconditional mirror of truth banished will be.*
*Days of silence will bare to the tree.*
*Death will be placed to the givers hand.*
*Figment of darkness will colden the land.*
*Set free the guilt of the darkness within.*

*Bear in mind, the CURSE has no sin.*

*Recite three times, not by the language of love.*
*Unity and light will release the dove.*
*"Tu Me Maques"*
*"Tu Me Maques"*
*"Tu Me Maques"*

"What does that mean?" her father asked. He paced back and forth. "What does that mean?"

She could feel his mounting panic. "It is French, but I have no clue what it means," she said, staring down at the paper. She rubbed her fingers gently over the silky texture. "But I know who does...Come on lets go back to my house."

Dee put everything back in the trunk, picked it up, and headed to her truck not waiting on her father. When she got to the truck she noticed he seemed reluctant to leave.

"We'll come back, I promise," Dee said softly. "Let's find out what this means first."

Like a child not wanting to leave the playground, he moved slowly and finally got into the truck.

## CHAPTER THIRTY-SIX
## You Are Missing From Me

*The unfolding of your words gives light; it gives understanding.* **Psalms 119:130**

*Lizzy, with that car phone idea, was right on the money, three times now. I could have used it again, today.*

Back at the house, Dee fought her way through the front door with the trunk in hand and set it on to the couch. She went to the phone

"BUCKETS. May I help you?" Lizzy's voice sang out.

"Hey Liz, didn't your grandmother teach you French?" Dee asked.

"She sure did, why?"

"What does 'Tu me maques' mean?"

"Easy," Lizzy giggled, "I miss you."

"I miss you...I miss you...I miss you," Dee said and nothing happened. Her father just stood in front of her waiting.

"Well, I miss you too." Lizzy laughed. "You are feeling better huh?" Lizzy giggled some more. "'Tu' is you. 'Me' really means, to me. 'Maques' means missing or lack of." Lizzy chatted on. "'You are missing from me.'"

"Thanks, Liz." Dee slammed the phone down, turned to her father and smiled.

"What?" he asked

"You are missing from me!" Dee yelled at her father and smiled.

"You are missing from me!" they yelled in unison.

"You are missing from me!" they yelled again in unison.

"You are missing from me!" he yelled and Dee's heart melted.

That was everything she ever needed to hear from him. That very moment, the trunk lid flew open and twenty doves flew out of it. The doves flew all around the room until Dee made her way to the door and opened it to allow them out into the world.

She stood on the front stoop with her hands held high, as if she had released the doves herself. She noticed Johnny watching her from across the street. She blew him a kiss and returned into the house.

"You are missing from me!" she whispered to her father.

"Not anymore." He smiled and held his daughter for the first time in many years. He grasped her face and stared in her eyes.

"That old house is yours Dee. You inherited it."

"It is?" she asked. "Well, hell Daddy, let's get some paint and fix her up then." Dee smiled.

They spent the next two days hammering old boards and cleaning windows and cob webs. They painted the outside and made her beautiful again.

Everything she ever dreamed about him paled in comparison to how wonderful he really was.

Back at her house after they cleaned up for the day, they talked over dinner of the songs he rocked her to sleep to.

"I remember that," she would say. "I remember us also hanging bottles on the limbs out on that aspen tree. Oh my God...just like the ones in that trunk." She glanced over her shoulder at the trunk that now peacefully rested on the floor.

"Yep, that was me," he said with a smile. "I told you...you are a Bishop and we have gifts," he said.

Dee stood and picked up her mother's journal as she cleaned up the kitchen table. The letter fell from it—she picked it up.

*Should I bother looking at this anymore? What could I possibly learn that he can't tell me himself? What the hell...*

Dee looked at her father who sat at her kitchen table and smiled. She took the letter from the envelope and read it out loud to her father.

> *To whom it may concern:*
>
> *Henry Bishop Sr. has been confirmed deceased on Dec 18, 1977 at 6:30am.*
>
> *The next of kin is entitled to all of the asset listed below:*
>
> *616 Railroad Blvd., Florida*
>
> *1484 Garden Lake Road, Florida*
>
> *No taxes are due on the addresses above until Dec 17, 2000. They were paid in full by insurance policy #CG22910.*

"How can this be?" she asked as she looked up from the letter that she held in her hand.

Her father no longer sat in the kitchen chair. Dee ran to the front window and looked out to the aspen tree. It looked as though he was lounging in the shade of the tree.

"We Bishops have gifts my dearest Dee," his voice rang out above her head.

The image faded and so did his voice. Dee sank like a rock into the couch as a tear rolled down her cheek, bewildered but blessed.

Then the sour stomach was back and forced her to dash to the bathroom.

*Haugggg!*

# CHAPTER THIRTY-SEVEN
## The Test

***Grief can take care of itself, but to get the full value of joy you must have somebody to divide it with.* Mark Twain**

That evening Dee returned to work and brought the letter along with her. Night shifts were going to be hard for her. She knew every night, at closing, she would be expecting her father to arrive, just as he did that fateful night.

Maybe bringing the letter with her was her way of staying normal. She walked through the front door. Lizzy turned and smiled as she excused herself from a customer and made her way to the end of the bar to meet Dee.

"How was your mini- vacation?" Lizzy asked. "When do I get to meet your father? Is he coming up tonight?"

Lizzy was full of questions. Dee pulled the letter from her back pack and handed it to her with a slight smile. She was not sure how to explain the beauty of it or the sadness. Besides, would Lizzy actually ever understand her gift? Or just accept it. *Let her figure it out.*

Lizzy opened the letter and read it. Confusion and shock covered her face. "Was this in that chest the whole time? Oh, Dee, I am so sorry. The good thing from this is that you have closure." Lizzy held the letter to her heart. "You shouldn't be here, you need to give yourself more time, Dee."

"I have had the best two days in my entire life, Lizzy. I'm ready to work again," she said as Lizzy wrapped her arms around her. "Really, I'm much better now."

"Are you sure?" Lizzy asked.

"Yes, I am sure," Dee said.

"Guess what? I got my period *again!"* Lizzy announced.

"I'm sorry Lizzy. I do know, if it's part of your fate, you just need patience. Maybe it just isn't your time for children," Dee said. Then she felt like her knees had turned to mush.

*Oh my God... I always get my period a week before Lizzy. That means I am late.* Dee felt the sour in her stomach return. Panic set in. *Could I be pregnant? This will kill Lizzy. Maybe that is why my father was saying we needed to break the curse quickly. Could he have known?*

"Dee, are you sure you are alright?" Lizzy asked, peering into Dee's face.

*She can see my worries.* "Yeah, yeah, just little tired is all. I'll be fine." Dee patted Lizzy's shoulder and hung her back pack on the hook.

"I'm starving what-cha got for special for today?" she asked, trying to filter her panic. She was careful to avoid eye contact with Lizzy.

"There is a big pot of Brunswick stew on the stove, go get you some. I'll hang out till you're ready to work," Lizzy said.

*Oh no this is probably the first time in my life I am wishing her away. This isn't right. Dear God, what should I do?*

"No, no," Dee said with a forced smile. "I'm good right now, I just was wondering, for later. You know me, always get the midnight munchies."

"Are you sure?" Lizzy didn't look convinced.

"Yes!" Dee insisted.

"Okay." Lizzy grabbed a bottle of wine and winked. "Gotta add a little zing to this baby making stuff." Lizzy smiled and shook the bottle of wine. "I do think we are trying too hard. Maybe the wine will make it fun and not so much like work." She grabbed her purse and slung it over her shoulder, then kissed Dee on the cheek. "Swear you'll call if you need me?"

"I swear!" Dee held her right hand up and smiled.

Dee watched as Lizzy, her bottle of wine in hand, pranced out of the front door. Dee exhaled all of the tension that had hit her in that moment of realization.

*My period is late. Shit! Shit! Shit!* Dee couldn't think, or have an intelligent conversation, so she just served, smiled and kept herself busy. Dee knew the customers noticed she wasn't herself, but she was too preoccupied to care. She was worried.

*I've put on weight. My stomach hasn't been right in a week or so.* Dee wiped the bar down several times not realizing that it was already clean. *Could I really be pregnant?* Dee looked up. The jukebox had quit playing and two customers sat staring at her.

"Gosh, I am sorry fellah's. I have a lot on my mind tonight," Dee apologized, realizing their bottles of beer sat empty. She collected the empties and replaced them with fresh, cold ones.

"Wanna talk about it?" one gentleman asked.

"Umm..." Dee then answered, "I never met my father, but I just found out he's deceased. I guess I'm still recovering from that news."

"Yeah, that's a tough one," he said as he sipped his beer.

"Yeah," Dee smiled. *And I could be pregnant. And my best friend has been trying to have a baby with her husband for a year now. And If I tell her... it is going to kill her.  And I have no idea what I need to do.* Dee just smiled her zip-lock smile.

The night finally ended and Dee was thankful but now she needed to desperately find out if she was pregnant. Since it was so late and nothing remained open in town, she drove all the way to the next town north to an all-night drug store to buy a pregnancy test.

Dee jumped back in her truck and stared at the brown paper bag. Dee grasped it tightly and prayed. *God please let me make the right decision. Whatever this test is... I know in my heart that it is my fate. I'm not asking for a solution, all I'm asking is for strength. Please show me the path and I will follow.*

Dee returned home and read the instruction sheet that she pulled from the pregnancy test box. It stated that for best results, morning urine should be used.

Even though she wanted to know the results almost as much as she'd wanted to find her father, Dee decided to follow the directions so she'd have no doubts about the results.

She went to her room, slipped into her jammies, crawled into bed and lay still for a moment. She placed her hand on her tummy and stared at the ceiling.

*There could be a baby in here.*

## CHAPTER THIRTY-EIGHT
### Decisions

***Each friend represents a world in us, a world possibly not born until they arrive, and it is only by this meeting that a new world is born.* Anais Nin**

*Dee awakened in the mystical forest underneath an aspen tree like the one her father rested peacefully under. She stood wiping the leaves that clung to her dress.*

*She spotted Lizzy crying in the distance between two trees. In the shadows of the trees Lizzy sat leaning against a willow tree, head tucked in her arms to hide her face. Dee moved closer to explain to her.*

*Everything, but nothing came to her at the same time. What did she need to say to her? Did she have questions or answers? Confusion swirled around her. Then the angry boy jumped out from behind one of the shadows.*

*"Found ya!" he said, without the sad or angry pout. Dee was startled. His distraction frustrated her though she couldn't understand why it would. Over the weeks she had become quite fond of him.*

*But now he intruded on her friendship with Lizzy. She looked again to find Lizzy but she was gone...*

It was morning. The sun peeked through the blinds of Dee's bedroom. Her eyes fluttered a bit, then she realized her blinds were down. *I don't remember shutting the blinds last night. I always leave them open.*

*Hmmm.* Dee sat up in her bed. *It is time to see if I'm pregnant.* Dee felt anticipation followed by dread. Similar to the feeling she had when opening the Raggedy Ann and Andy chest for the first time or when she and Lizzy opened BUCKETS.

*Lizzy can't be here with me for this one. I will face this alone.* Dee squared her shoulders and marched to the bathroom. She removed the stick from the packaging and stared for a moment.

Once she was finished, she returned the stick to the original packaging. She concealed it from herself until she was ready to look and know the answer. She set it on the bathroom counter and proceeded to the kitchen.

Dee made herself a cup of tea and sat at the kitchen table. Her mother's journal still lay just as she had left it. She picked it up and opened it to a random page.

*April 20, 1977*

*I received a letter today from a lawyer out of Tennessee. What I had feared all along, has happened. My dearest Henry Sr. is now in heaven with his son. I have dreaded this moment, but always knew it was coming. According to the newspaper clipping he was traveling with a carnival group, they travelled towns across the east coast. He was found dead in his camper. He drank himself to death. The carnival group was headed south to do the Florida tour. He may have been trying to make his way back to us, but that will never be known.*

*The girls, Dee and Gina, are adjusted to the fact they have no father. Although Dee has recently starting talking to herself again. I have decided to get her help and some counseling. I have been told children tend to fill voids with imaginary friends, but this is different. She is calling him Daddy. I worry a great deal for my daughters, and I will do whatever is possible so they too can survive their fate.*

*My dearest Henry and Henry Jr., may God forever hold you in his arms. Nurture you with love that this world was unable to do.*

Dee closed the journal, laid it back on the table and sipped her tea. *Okay Dee, let's see your fate.*

She walked to the bathroom, picked up the box, hesitated, then slowly pulled out the stick. She looked at it and a tear rolled down her cheek. She wasn't sure if she was happy or sad.

The stick read positive. Yep, she was pregnant. *I don't even know what his name was. Should I even consider keeping this baby? Is this why my father finally came back? Is this my fate?* All types of questions popped in and out of her head. *I can't tell Lizzy. It will kill her. I need to weigh out my options.*

Dee went back into her kitchen and picked up a phone book. She thumbed through the pages to find the closest women's clinic. *I could just go and talk to them. I still have some time. Why? Why me? I am not the mother type. Lizzy needs this. Not me! God what were you thinking?* Anger started to consume her. Dee crumbled to her knees and started to cry, then folded her hands and prayed.

"Dear God *please* let me make the right decision! I can't hurt Lizzy! She saved my life! This will crush her!" Dee screamed in anger.

She stood and stomped angrily to her room babbling, "I know what I need to do. I know what has to happen. I can't have a baby. I'm too young for this. What about BUCKETS? I can't imagine a pregnant woman behind a bar." Dee continued mumbling her irrational thoughts as she dressed. "Just go get it taken care of and forget it ever happened."

# CHAPTER THIRTY-NINE
## Reflections

*The boundaries which divide Life from Death are at best shadowy and vague. Who shall say where one ends, and where the other begins?* **Edgar Allen Poe**

Dee drove around for hours in a numbed state. Not one coherent thought of any kind until her eighth drive-by of the women's clinic.

She decided to pull into the parking lot. Thoughts flooded her at once. *I can just go in and get information. The cost? How long do I have to decide? Adoption is out of the question. I can't go through a whole pregnancy and hand my baby to someone. Oh God and Lizzy...Why God? Why is this happening to me?* Dee banged her head on the steering wheel. *I really don't need this!*

Dee sat for a moment squeezing her eyes tight to keep the tears from falling onto her cheeks. She rolled down the truck window to get a breath of fresh air. She glanced in the rearview mirror of the truck and saw children playing in a daisy field.

She moved closer to the mirror to get a better look. The children were chasing butterflies. Dee snapped her head around to see without the reflection and only buildings surrounded her.

She searched the whole perimeter of the parking lot—no field of daisies.

She closed her eyes and exhaled. *What is happening to me?* She opened her eyes and prepared to go into the clinic. She glanced to her right and in her passenger seat of her truck sat the angry boy, *smiling* and holding up one finger. A beautiful blue Butterfly fluttered on the tiny tip. He turned to her and smiled. It was the most beautiful smile she had ever seen. She felt instant love for the child. A love that was untouchable to the rest of the world. A love that no words could define. A precious love. A love that could do no wrong. A love that saw no faults.

The butterfly flew off the boy's finger, breaking the spell she seemed to be under, fluttered past her head and out the window. Her gaze followed its bouncy flight. She turned back to the passenger seat and the angry boy's smile had turned back to the grimace. He crossed his arms and slowly faded away.

"No wait!" she yelled reaching out to touch him. She sat upright in the truck. She noticed a young girl, much younger than she was, being wheeled out in a wheel chair. They wheeled her to a car with a young male that held open the passenger door for her. She watched as a nurse and the young man helped the girl into the car.

*This baby will never know his father.*

"I can't do this! I can't do this! I can't do this!" Dee cried as she banged her head each time on the steering wheel, her finger curled so tightly around the wheel that her knuckles were white.

"Ma'am? Are you all right?" a gentle voice said from outside the window. Dee turned her head to see it was the nurse that had been helping the young couple to the car.

"As a matter of fact, I...I...I'm not," she stuttered. Dee was never good at allowing herself to be seen as weak, but today she was out of reserves. She was at a horrible cross road.

She was more scared of hurting Lizzy than of having a child or even raising it herself. *Lizzy so desperately wants a child.* The fear of never loving someone as much as loving that child; the fear of not being a good mother. *Lizzy would be a perfect mother.*

"Maybe there is something I can help you with?" the nurse asked.

"I'm pregnant!" Dee blurted as a tear rolled down her cheek. She quickly wiped it away.

"I'll be back," the nurse said.

Moments later, she returned with a few pamphlets of different avenues to take.

"Here take these, read them over. You have many options. There is even a hotline to talk to a counselor. Honey, please just take your time to consider what you want, but take it from me, I have been in your shoes and ten years later I am still battling my regret."

The nurse walked away and glanced back before re-entering the clinic. Dee wiped the tears from her face, then cranked up the truck and put it in reverse. She pulled away from the clinic.

On the drive home she thought back to the children playing in the daisy field and how she'd felt seeing the angry boy's smile. She thought about the smell of babies and how they bring about that true feeling of unconditional love.

She even started designing the baby's room in her mind. Of course, Ripley's old room would be perfect, and it was the closest to her room. *Only if I decide to have this baby, of course.*

She knew that breaking Lizzy's heart was her main concern. She'd lost everyone she ever loved, except for Ripley and Lizzy. She didn't want to lose Lizzy's friendship, but she didn't think she could kill her child to keep it, either.

*I need to just tell her. I can't keep it from her. Being lied to is worse than living with the truth. Having a baby isn't deceitful, but deceiving is.*

"Truth is a powerful state of being. It is real and holds no guilt, no matter how much it hurts," Dee announced.

"I'll tell her everything, even the fact that I am considering an abortion, too. *Then* I won't feel forced into doing something I'm not sure I want to do," Dee told her reflection in the rearview mirror.

# CHAPTER FORTY
## Determination

***True friendship is like sound health: the value of it is seldom known until it be lost.* Charles Caleb Colton**

Over the next two days Dee avoided contact with Lizzy. It wasn't so hard since Lizzy was sure Dee needed time to grieve her father coming and going from her life and Gracey and Angel were both around to help run things at BUCKETS.

Dee needed to get her words right in her head. Drinking beer had always helped, but *if,* and only *if* she decided to keep this baby, it wouldn't be good for him or her.

She knew Lizzy would be at BUCKETS this morning cooking up the special of the day and Gracey would be there to open, so today was the day she would go and talk to Lizzy. Her heart pounded in her chest as she drove. *I can do this.*

Dee pulled into the parking lot. Just as she suspected Lizzy was there. *I can do this.*

She got out and looked up at the sign that read BUCKETS. *We did this together. Lizzy did this with me and for me. I can't have this baby. Buckets was my dream, not hers.* Somehow, the sign BUCKETS had suddenly changed the thoughts and words she wanted to say. Dee turned to go back to the truck and leave to get her thoughts straight again. The click of the front door lock stopped her in her tracts.

"Hey!"

Dee stopped moving and didn't turn.

"You aren't working in your garden on your day off?" Lizzy sang out through the door.

"Nooo." Dee hesitated with her back still turned. "Can we talk?" Dee asked as she spun around.

Dee saw fear reflected on Lizzy's face. At that moment, Dee knew this was a day she might never forget.

"Are you alright Dee? You are scaring me! Come inside!" Lizzy now looked even more nervous.

Dee walked through the doors and then chattered her way to the kitchen acting like nothing was wrong. "What did you make today?" Dee put her nose to the air and sniffed.

"Chicken and dumplings." Lizzy stopped, put her hands on her hips. "What is it Dee?" she demanded.

Dee stopped and without turning, said, "I need to tell you something that may harm our friendship and I don't know how to say it."

"What?" Lizzy gasped. "Just say it!" Lizzy insisted, hands still on her hips.

"I am pregnant."

Dee turned to face Lizzy. Lizzy's head dropped along with her hands from her hips as she deflated. Her legs looked as though she was going to crumble. Her hands became shaky and her bottom lip tucked underneath her teeth. Dee knew Lizzy was about to cry. She remembered that look well.

That was the same look she'd had when Lizzy found out Lee, her high school sweetheart, was going to marry another women. Or, when Lizzy's grandma was on her death bed. *How can I do this to her?*

Dee shook her head. "Lizzy, I am going to have an abortion," Dee cried out hoping to change Lizzy's reaction. Nothing changed but the silence became thicker. Lizzy turned without a word, then slowly walked out the door.

"Dear God, why have you done this to me?" Dee yelled into the air. She pulled out a bar stool and sat down, cried desperately unto her hands, hoping, praying and looking for answers.

All of this... Everything she had been through this past year, the loneliness, seeing Gina, the chest, her mother's journal, her father, and the angry boy. *Henry Jr., what was it he said? Whatever you think it is- it isn't.*

Dee stood, walked to the paper towel dispenser, grabbed a paper towel and dried her face. She moved to the kitchen and stood in front of Lizzy's simmering pot of Chicken and Dumplings. *Lizzy would be a wonderful mother-not me.*

"Hello!" a voice called, which startled Dee from her thoughts. It was Gracey. Dee glided out of the kitchen and made an appearance.

"No Lizzy today?" Gracey asked as she hung her purse on the coat hook.

"Ohhh, she had to run out. I think... I pissed her off," Dee said. *Tough as nails I am.* "Gracey I would really appreciate it if you could watch over BUCKETS today, and make sure Angel is okay tonight. Lizzy and I need to work out some issues," Dee confessed.

"Is everything okay?" Gracey looked concerned.

"I'll make sure it is...okay." Dee marched toward the front door.

"I have BUCKETS under control. You do what you need to do. I've always said I am here for you girls," Gracey said. Dee never stopped and didn't turn around.

"Thank you, Gracey, that means a lot."

## CHAPTER FORTY-ONE
## Magical Garden

*A true friend is someone who knows the song in your heart, and can sing it back to you when you have forgotten the words."* **Author Unknown**

Dee drove around a bit. She wondered if she should go out to Lizzy's house or just give her some time. She decided when Lizzy was ready to talk, she'd let Dee know.

Lizzy always held her feelings in or wrote them down. Dee knew that and wondered if she would be getting a letter from her, or a note at least.

Whatever Lizzy was thinking or feeling only she would know how to work them out. It was all over now. No matter how it ended, the right thing had been done and the truth was out.

Although she felt horrible, another part of her felt great relief. She'd faced her worst fear and was honest with Lizzy anyway. Dee decided to go home. *BUCKETS will be fine today.*

Her garden needed tending, so that was what she would do- for today at least. The garden always seemed to help her work out her thoughts and settle her self-destructive mode.

She got out of the truck, biting her nails as she always did when life twisted around her plans. Dee bypassed the house and walked straight to the garden.

"Hi," a teary voice rang from the swing. Dee looked up and there sat Lizzy.

"Hi." Dee walked over and sat next to her friend. Silence danced between them for moments.

"I came here to see if my eagle was here," Lizzy whispered and a tear rolled down her cheek. "He wasn't." Her voice cracked.

"Please Lizzy, don't be mad at me!" Dee stopped the swing with her foot. "I can't lose you, I need you. You gave me life and hope," Dee cried out. Nothing but silence surrounded them a few moments more.

"Dee... I'm not mad at you...I..." Lizzy broke down in an uncontrollable cry. Dee stared at the top of the tall pine where Lizzy's eagle used to perch. *Please help us!*

The eagle swooped down at that very moment and settled on the branch.

"He is here now, Liz," Dee whispered.

Lizzy looked up and then something caught her attention. She was sniffing the air. Dee too smelled the air- *roses.*

"Do you smell it, Dee?" Lizzy asked through the sniffles and tears.

"I do." Dee smiled. "See the butterflies?" Dee pointed

"And the eagle," Lizzy whispered. They sat in the swing waiting for answers to emerge from their cluttered minds.

A smile slowly spread across Lizzy's face. "I love you Dee, I'm not mad at *you.*" Lizzy stopped the swing with her foot this time.

"I *am* angry. That is why I'm so upset. I am angry *I'm* not pregnant. I am angry, that *you* are. I'm angry... that I *am* angry. I'm being selfish and *that* angers me, too."

She started the swing with a push of her foot. "I came here because this is where it all began. So...I guess I figured if I was here, it wouldn't end." Lizzy's lip tucked under her teeth again. The creaking of the swing's chains filled the minutes of silence.

"I don't know what to do, Liz," Dee pleaded after they swung a few more times.

"Dee, that baby needs you. You need that baby," Lizzy whispered as a tear rolled again down her cheek. "And...I need you, too." Lizzy's voice went two octaves higher. "You can't have an abortion." Lizzy inhaled. "I'm not telling you what to do. I just believe that no matter what curve balls life throws at us, there's a purpose. It has a reason. It is part of the plan that God has for us."

"Yeah, I know." Moments passed. "Part of me desperately wants this child, Lizzy," Dee admitted. They watched the butterflies.

"So keep it," Lizzy whimpered. They resumed swinging and the creaking was as rhythmic as a Grandfather clock.

Dee noticed the cockle plant hadn't come back up. *I finally got rid of that damn plant once and for all.*

"Can I be Godmother at least?" Lizzy nudged Dee and brought her back.

"Damn straight." Dee smiled back.

Once again comfortable silence wrapped around the two of them as they enjoyed the magical garden. Each would glance over and smile at one another. They spent the better part of the afternoon there.

Lizzy jerked up from the seat in a panic. "We need to find more help at BUCKETS!"

"Whoa, whoa, I'm pregnant Liz, not dead."

## CHAPTER FORTY-TWO
### Humbling

*It is not so much our friends' help that helps us as the confident knowledge that they will help us.* **Epicurus, Greek philosopher**

Days turned into weeks and weeks into months. The summer was gone and so was a good portion of the fall. Lizzy kept a close eye on Dee and tried not to worry about that stubborn streak. And, she made peace with the idea that it wasn't her time to have children.

Dee's belly grew bigger by the day. She fought for every work shift that she could. She would plead, "BUCKETS was *my* dream! I'm not going to desert ya'll!"

Lizzy had hired a couple more girls because she knew Dee would try to work until the end, which concerned her for the baby's health as well as Dee's.

"You only have a month or so left, Dee. You need to start taking things easy," Lizzy begged.

She hung around after her shift to clean or decorate for the current holiday just to watch and make sure that Dee's stubbornness didn't get the best of her.

Sure enough, it happened one afternoon. Lizzy was in the kitchen organizing and cleaning. She'd told Dee that it was the time of the year that the state inspector would be coming around. When she poked her head out into the bar area, Lizzy noticed Dee had become sluggish and disoriented. Her speech seemed very slow.

"Dee, are you feeling okay?" Lizzy asked. She noticed Dee had a puffy look about her face and then remembered back when her sister Lynn was pregnant with her first baby, that wasn't a good sign.

"Just a little tired, is all," Dee said as she made her way to a stool to sit down. Lizzy worked her way to the soda cooler, where they kept bottles of water and grabbed a bottle to take to Dee.

"My stomach is cramping a little. Probably because I haven't sat down in a while." Dee rubbed her hands over her belly that poked out over her lap.

"That isn't sounding good, Dee. Maybe you should call your doctor and ask. I'll call if you would like," Lizzy offered knowing damn well Dee would try to blow it off.

"Would you?" Dee asked.

At that moment, Lizzy knew Dee wasn't feeling right. Otherwise she'd have insisted Lizzy stop fussing over her. Her panic surged.

"Sure I will," Lizzy calmly answered back.

Fighting her normal tendency to completely panic, Lizzy took a breath. *I'll call Gracey to come in first. Then I'll call the doctor.* She smiled at Dee and walked to the phone.

"Gracey? Hey, it's Lizzy. Can you come up to work for Dee?" She kept a slight smile on her face, not wanting to alarm Dee.

"No, no. Yeah, I was going to call him, and see what he suggested. Gosh, thank you so much." Lizzy hung up the phone.

Despite the fact that she and Gracey knew the day would come when Dee couldn't be on her feet so much, Lizzy was still surprised, and worried that Dee still didn't seem to be aware of where she was. She sat rubbing her belly, as if no one else existed.

Lizzy quickly picked up the receiver and dialed Dee's doctor's office.

"Hi, I am calling with regards to Dee Bishop. She is eight months pregnant. She isn't feeling well." Lizzy glanced at Dee again and turned away so Dee would not see or hear Lizzy's concern.

Lizzy spoke slowly and softly. "She looks very puffy and her words sound slightly slurred. She also said her stomach is cramping. She is a very stubborn woman and wouldn't want me to call unless it was very serious. I'm really worried." Lizzy glanced again at Dee, who still looked like she was in her own world.

"Yes ma'am, that doesn't sound good. Give her water to drink," the nurse said.

"I did," Lizzy answered. She could hear the nurse discussing Dee's symptoms with someone in the back ground.

"Bring her to our birthing center so the doctor can check her out," the nurse said when she un-muffled the phone.

"Is it serious?" Lizzy asked.

"Could be. She may just be dehydrated. That's why he wants to see her. At her last visit, her blood pressure was borderline high and it could be that," the nurse said calmly. "Do not let her drive."

"No ma'am, I am bringing her," Lizzy announced. *Wow, they know Dee is stubborn too.* Lizzy got a clean towel, wet it, and took it over to Dee and placed it on her forehead. "How you feeling?" Lizzy asked.

"Not good. I can't think, Liz," Dee mumbled. "Did you get a hold of the doctor?"

"I did. He wants to see you. Gracey is coming in and I can take you." Lizzy noticed Dee's slurring was getting worse.

"Good. I *really* don't feel good," Dee whispered. Customers were watching and they too looked concerned. "Liz?"

"Yeah, Dee? I'm here." Lizzy wiped her forehead with the cold cloth that felt warm from the heat of Dee's body.

"I'm scared," Dee mumbled.

"I'm here, Dee. I'll make sure you get taken care of okay?" Lizzy soothed with words although she was scared too. Something was very wrong.

Several minutes later Gracey showed and took over BUCKETS. She helped Lizzy get Dee to her truck. Lizzy hopped into the driver's seat and cautiously sped out of the parking lot and directly to the birthing center.

## CHAPTER FORTY-THREE
Surrender

*Wait, my daughter, until you learn how the matter turns out.* **Ruth 3:18**

Lizzy whipped the truck into the closest spot she could find to the door, jumped out, and ran to the entrance of the birthing center, leaving Dee in the truck.

Close to full blown panic, Lizzy searched the lobby looking for a nurse or someone to help her get Dee into the clinic. Dee was almost unconscious which made Lizzy even more of a wreck.

She spotted a woman behind the desk near the center of the room. "Excuse me, I need assistance with a pregnant woman. She isn't strong enough to walk in. I need a wheel chair, a nurse, something!" Lizzy nearly screamed.

The woman nodded, picked up the telephone received, pressed a button and spoke to someone. She placed her hand over the phone then asked Lizzy, "What's the name?" in a monotone voice.

"Dee Bishop. Doctor Case sent us here," Lizzy hissed.

The women repeated Lizzy words into the phone then nodded toward someone behind Lizzy. Lizzy turned and a nurse was coming out of some swinging doors with a wheel chair. "Dee Bishop?"

"Yes, yes this way." Lizzy turned and headed back out the doors to the parking lot to retrieve Dee.

Lizzy and the nurse got Dee into the wheel chair and rolled her to the birthing center. Dee looked up at Lizzy who walked beside her wheel chair.

"No matter what Liz... the baby comes first," Dee said slowly.

Lizzy had no clue what Dee meant, but nodded and smiled. While Lizzy stood off to the side, the nurses got Dee set up in what they called a monitoring room, where several neatly made beds sat waiting to be filled. The nurse put little sticky tabs on Dee's belly, then wrapped a belt around her swollen belly. She ordered the other nurse to start an IV.

"She looks dehydrated," the head nurse announced as she wrapped Dee's arm with a blood pressure cuff.

"Is she going to be alright?" Lizzy asked.

"I fine," Dee slurred. "Just tired."

"Honey, she is here now, and in good hands. Just let us see what's going on," the nurse explained, as she took Dee's vitals.

Lizzy noticed Dee's feet were very swollen. She made her way to the bed and pulled Dee's shoes off one by one. Another nurse entered the room with what appeared to be the IV.

"We need to get her on some oxygen, now! The baby seems distressed," the head nurse ordered the IV nurse. "Call Doctor Case, and tell him her pressure is very high and her fever is increasing. The baby is showing a fast heart rate."

Lizzy knew something serious was happening. Dee looked as though she wasn't aware of the crisis. The IV nurse left the room quickly. Moments later she returned. "He said he is on his way and we may need to take the baby."

The head nurse put the oxygen mask over Dee's face and waved Lizzy over. "I need you to help me get her on her left side, honey."

Lizzy and the nurse turned Dee onto her side. Lizzy let her hand rest on Dee's hip, the touch helping her to fend off her panic.

The nurse watched the monitor that Lizzy assumed measured the baby's heart rate. Slowly it started to look less like a bunch of jumbled spaghetti and turned into a slower, organized line.

"That did it," the nurse said, giving Lizzy a pat on the shoulder.

"What is happening?" Lizzy asked.

"The baby's heart rate was speeding up which means he was stressed. Usually that means they aren't getting enough oxygen or the cord could be around his neck." The nurse explained. "He is stable, now. But the worry is getting his mother stable. Her blood pressure is very high. If we don't get that controlled it could be very dangerous for her," she said as she started setting up the IV in Dee's arm. She asked the other nurse to get Labatol to inject into the IV.

"What is that?" Lizzy asked.

"It's medication to lower the blood pressure," the nurse replied.

"Will that hurt the baby?" Lizzy asked, understanding now what Dee had meant about the baby coming first.

"No, it's given to pregnant women all the time, to control their pressure. Honey, we will make sure both mother and baby are fine. I promise," the nurse soothed.

Many moments later, Doctor Case entered the room. He looked around at all the machines and wrote notes in the file. "Lizzy?" he asked when he looked up.

"Yes?" She stood from the chair that sat next to Dee's bed.

"She has you listed on her paperwork as next of kin. She filled out papers. That means you have say in any treatment Ms. Bishop should or shouldn't undergo."

"Okay," Lizzy answered because she had no clue what Dee would need to undergo.

"As of right now we have Dee stable, and the baby as well, but we may need to take this baby using an emergency C-section, and if we don't, we could lose them both. She has written here, that if we have to decide which one to save... It should be the child." The doctor referred to his notes again, then glanced at Lizzy for any comment.

"Okay," Lizzy repeated again. *Oh God, why should I be the one agreeing to this?* Dee lay peacefully on her side sleeping due to the heavy dose of blood pressure medicine they had given her.

"This baby is at a very crucial time in his development. This is when the lung are developing. Its chance of survival are not good if we take him now," Doctor Case explained.

"I see," Lizzy said and slowly dropped into the chair. *I could lose them both... Dee said the baby comes first.* She cleared her throat. "What needs to happen?" Lizzy looked up at the doctor.

"If we can keep her in this bed, and in the hospital for..." He looked at his chart then finished. "Another week or two, then there is a chance we can save the baby."

"What about Dee?" Lizzy asked.

"We need to watch her pressure and keep getting urine samples to make sure her organs aren't shutting down. The liver is the first to go," the doctor explained. "You see, she has a severe case of pre-eclampsia/toxemia. It happens to many women. But, Dee needs to stay in bed until we can deliver this baby safely," he said, then looked at his nurse and nodded.

"Okay, then that's what we need to do," Lizzy ordered.

"Can we get her moved to a private room, as soon as possible?" he asked the nurse with a nod.

"I will see what I can do," she answered and turned toward the exit door, leaving Lizzy to watch Dee sleep peacefully.

Lizzy knew Dee's stubbornness would have fought the idea of bed rest, but she'd said *the baby comes first*. Lizzy was positive she was making the right choice for Dee and the baby.

*I can't lose them.*

## Chapter Forty-four
## Faith

*Some friends play at friendship, but a true friend sticks closer than one's nearest kin.* **Proverbs 18:24**

Once they had Dee moved into her private room and things seemed to be stable, Lizzy went out to the pay phone just outside of the birthing center.

She called Joe first to explain what was happening. Of course, Joe was ready to join Lizzy but she had to insist he stayed home to tend the house and the animals. She also asked him to check on Dee's house and the Garden for the next few days.

Next, Lizzy called Gracey and explained the situation. Gracey was more than understanding, and was quick to let her know that BUCKETS would be fine in their absence. That too was a relief. Lizzy exhaled a sigh of disbelief as thoughts invaded her brain.

Last, she phoned Ripley and explained everything Doctor Case had said word for word. And thought back to the day she had phoned Ripley about Dee's suicide attempt. This go round Ripley was unable to join her.

*I can't believe this is happening. Why? I just need to be strong for Dee. I can't let anything happen to Dee, no matter how strong willed she becomes.*

Lizzy made her way back through the automatic doors, and into the elevator that deposited her on Dee's floor. Lizzy sat by her side the whole week. Every time she dozed off, the automatic blood pressure machine would go off and startle her.

Ripley stopped in on her lunch breaks but was never able to stay very long.

Dee would awaken every so often to ask what was happening, and her pressure would go up. Not long after that, a nurse would enter the room and dose her up with more medicines. They occasionally mumbled, "Let's see if this one will work."

It was like they were running out of blood pressure meds to use to regulate Dee's pressure. That worried Lizzy even more.

"Liz?" Dee rasped every now and then.

"I'm still here, Dee," Lizzy replied as she reached for her hand.

"The curse is gone. The baby comes first," Dee mumbled. Lizzy rubbed Dee's hand and smiled as brightly as she could.

"Girl, we are gonna be fine. The doctor is just wanting you to rest, honey." *We can get through this.*

Then Dee went back to sleep and Lizzy sat with the sounds of the monitors softly beeping until she stopped noticing them.

At the start of week two, on occasion the nurses entered and put the oxygen mask over Dee's face and rolled her to her left side. That was Lizzy's signal that the baby's heart rate must have increased again. They took several urine samples a day from Dee. Things weren't getting better that was for sure. Still Lizzy kept hoping it would all be fine.

Then it finally happened, at the end of that long worry-some week. Lizzy sat by Dee's bed side and watched as a nurse left the room with another of Dee's urine samples.

The sudden, urgent beeping of the machines and the pressure monitor alarm sounded as though the world was ending. Lizzy got to her feet, her heart pounding in her chest as though it would fly out.

Into the room rushed at least six nurses. They started to turn Dee over, and not just onto her side but they had her onto all fours. Lizzy moved away from the bed to allow them to do their job.

"Call the Doctor! We can't get her or baby stable!" yelled out a nurse.

"Call the anesthesia department! We need to get this baby!" another nurse yelled over top of the beeping machines.

"Start prep now!" the nurse with the clipboard yelled.

Lizzy watched as they rolled Dee onto her back, pulled the gown up and started cleaning her belly. At that moment a gurney entered and they hoisted Dee onto it. They rolled her through the doors like a huge wave of white.

"We are losing her!" Lizzy heard the voices fade down the hall. She walked out into the hall as Dee vanished from sight.

She crumbled to her knees. Joe came from around the corner holding flowers from Dee's garden in his hand. He dropped the flowers to the floor as he made his way to Lizzy.

"Lizzy?" he asked as he scooped her up.

"Joe, they were losing her... the baby...I can't lose her, Joe!" Lizzy babbled. Joe tucked Lizzy neatly into his strong arms and cradled her head.

"I got you, Lizzy," he whispered as he noticed a nurse coming back down the hall.

"The baby is fine. We have lost the mother," one nurse said to another.

Lizzy and Joe slowly melted down the wall as though they had no bones, and landed on the floor.

Joe held Lizzy with everything he had, as they both fell apart, together.

## CHAPTER FORTY-FIVE
## Mystical Forest

*I will give a white stone, and on the white stone is written a new name that no one knows except the one who receives it. Revelations 2:17*

*I'm here...It's the mystical forest. Is he here?*

*Dee walked slowly between the trees searching for the angry boy just as she had always done, looking around each tree she passed. Beautifully lighted lanterns hung from the trees, shining enough for her to notice the muck on the ground was gone.*

*"He's not here anymore. He's made it to the daisy field," said a young boy's voice as he stepped out from behind an ash tree. It was Henry Jr., her brother.*

*"Henry?" Dee asked.*

*"It's me." He smiled.*

*"Where are we?"*

*"Half way," he answered kicking at some stones that seemed to be stuck in the ground. "The others are on their way," he said as he looked up at Dee.*

*"Others?" Dee asked.*

*"Mommy, Daddy, Gina. And your friends Raymond, Brad and some old guy named Roscoe."*

*What does this mean? She thought.*

*"We can only meet you here, in the mystical forest, now that the curse has been broken. If you go any further, you cannot return," he explained.*

*"Return?"*

*"Hey, Dee." A young girl's voice giggled from behind a beech tree.*

*"Gina?" Dee asked when she saw the face peek around the side of the tree.*

*"Yep!" Gina giggled, then she skipped towards Dee and Henry Jr.*

*"Where are Mom and Dad?" Dee asked.*

*"We are here, too!" Their voices in unison rang from behind a fir tree.*

*They stepped out and joined the group.*

*"We wanted to see you," her mother said. "You are so beautiful. We're so proud of you."*

*Dee looked over her mother's shoulder and saw Raymond, Brad and the old man Roscoe in the distance, standing between an orange and a lemon tree. The three of them waved.*

*"Why won't they join us?" Dee asked.*

*"They are only allowed to that point, Dee. They're not of your blood," her mother explained.*

*Her father looked better than she ever remembered. He smiled at her and spread out his hands. "The love of God is unconditional. He expects nothing but love from you, or any of us, in return. You cannot make the wrong choices. They are all in the plan," he said.*

*Then Gina spoke. "You have to decide Dee."*

*"Decide what?" she asked.*

*"If you are coming with us or going back," Henry Jr. contributed.*

*"Going back to what?" Dee asked.*

*"To your baby," her mother whispered with a smile.*

"We have her back!" A woman's voice rang out and Dee's eyes fluttered. Bright lights surrounded her along with people of all sorts working like busy bees.

"Let's get her sewn back up," Doctor Case coached.

"She's stable!" another voice said.

"Hi," the nurse said to Dee interrupting all the background chatter. She moved Dee's hair from her face. "You gave us quite a scare. Would you like to see your baby boy?" she asked, smiling.

Dee's throat was dry and she said, "yes", but no sound came out. The nurse must have understood her because she re-appeared holding the most beautiful baby Dee had ever seen. He was so tiny. The nurse held him gently with two hands, but could have easily only used one.

"He is healthy as a horse. We just need to get some food in him and fatten him up. Sometimes toxemia babies get deprived of nutrients." The nurse smiled at Dee. "Once they get you all buttoned up and in a better bed we can let you hold him."

"He's beautiful," Dee groaned. "I want to name him Henry Bishop the Third," she whispered. "To carry on the family name."

Then she dozed off into a peaceful sleep.

# CHAPTER FORTY_SIX
## Welcome Henry

*I will give you treasures of darkness and riches hidden in secret places.* **Isaiah 45:3**

Lizzy and Joe held each other as tightly as they were capable of doing. Lizzy prayed over and over. *Please God, stay with her.*

After thirty long minutes, the double doors opened and out walked the head nurse. Lizzy and Joe stared at her as they rose from the floor where they'd been huddled since they'd overheard the surgical nurse.

"Baby is healthy," the nurse said. "It's a boy."

"How's Dee?" Lizzy asked, afraid of what the answer might be.

"Mom is still in the danger zone but we got her back. We're on top of it," the nurse explained.

*She's alive! Thank you, God!* "When can we see her?" Lizzy asked. She turned to Joe.

He smiled as he wiped the tears from her face.

"Soon. We'll be moving her to recovery and the baby back to this room." She pointed to the door way of Dee's hospital room. "She gave us quite a scare, though."

*Yeah, that's my Dee.* Always keeping people on their toes, Lizzy thought as she and Joe re-entered the room that was once occupied by Dee. Now all that had changed. It was now to be occupied by the Bishop *family*.

Again Lizzy smiled at Joe as he reached and clutched her hand as if he was thankful for what he had.

* * *

After Lizzy paced the room several times in anticipation, the baby boy was rolled into the room. Fresh linens and fresh beginnings floated about the room.

"Baby needs to eat." A nurse followed carrying bottles into the room. She handed them to Lizzy. "Mom can't breast feed. She won't be out of recovery for a while and won't be strong enough to feed and burp. Plus, she's still on medication." She smiled at Lizzy.

"Looks as though you are this baby's mommy for now," the nurse said to Lizzy. She handed Lizzy the bottle, then picked the baby up and put him into Lizzy arms.

"Sit," she said and moved the chair under Lizzy's bottom. Joe watched smiling from ear to ear.

Oh, how beautiful he was. His tiny hands poked their way out of the blanket, which was tightly wrapped around his tiny body. Lizzy smiled and butterflies darted about in her belly.

She glanced at Joe, who had a tear rolling down his face. She knew how much he longed for children and she understood his tear.

Lizzy glanced at baby and back at Joe who gave her a wink followed by a smile. She rubbed the nipple on the bottle across the baby's mouth until he suddenly latched on.

"See, you're a natural," the nurse said and left the room.

Lizzy was the first to hold and feed him. Then came the first diaper. Lizzy and Joe had to figure that one out on their own, and the nurse laughed them through it.

After spending a few weeks in the hospital, Dee was able to return home. She still had to stay in bed, but that was nothing. Lizzy, Joe and sometimes Ripley helped out with the feedings, and changings.

Lizzy cooked up good food for Dee, to help get her strength back.

As for Dee, she was grateful. She was home with her new family member-Henry Bishop III.

## Epilogue

*The moment that you died*
*my heart was torn in two,*
*one side filled with heartache,*
*the other died with you.*

*I often lie awake at night,*
*when the world is fast asleep, and*
*take a walk down memory lane,*
*with tears upon my cheeks.*

*Remembering you is easy,*
*I do it every day,*
*but missing you is heartache*
*that never goes away.*

*I hold you tightly within my heart*
*and there you will remain.*
*Until the joyous day arrives,*
*that we will meet again. -* **Unknown**

**O you who dwell in the gardens, my companions are listening for your voice; let me hear it.**
**Song of Solomon 8:13**

*Six months later*

"Come on Henry," Dee fussed as she wiped up applesauce from the highchair that he sat in. "It goes into the mouth. Like this. Ummm," Dee coached as she put a big spoon of apple sauce into her own mouth. Then she scooped up more and aimed it at the baby's mouth. He smacked it away. Apple sauce spewed everywhere and Henry laughed.

Someone knocked at the door. Dee yelled, "Come in!"

Lizzy made her way to the kitchen, where the Bishop family resided. "Hey!"

"Hey. I can't get him to eat. He keeps slapping it from my hand," Dee said in frustration.

"He thinks you are playing with him. Let me try." Lizzy pulled up a chair and sat it directly in front of Henry.

"Let's eat." Lizzy faked like she was eating. She did it a few more times, not attempting to give him any. "I've had this strange craving for pancakes made with applesauce like my grandma use to make me," Lizzy said to Dee with a smirk.

"Um,Um," Henry babbled.

Lizzy then turned the spoon. He opened his mouth and took the mouthful in.

"Oh my God. He did it! He did it!" Dee bounced up and down.

"He just needed to know that...this was what he was supposed to do." Lizzy smirked again as she scooped another spoonful and fed it to Henry.

"You are going to be such a good mom, Liz," Dee said.

"That's why I am *here,* Dee." She turned to Dee and gave her a little smile.

"I know you are a super godmother. This mommy stuff is hard work," Dee mumbled.

"I'm pregnant," Lizzy blurted out, now flashing a hundred-watt smile.

"Really?" Dee squeaked.

"Really."

Lizzy stood and the two of them danced around the kitchen as Henry Bishop III giggled with a toothless, applesauce smile.

## Gifts of Trees

Throughout the existence of man, trees have had symbolic meanings in every culture, religion, and social groups.

Christian's have the Tree of Knowledge. Buddhist's, the Tree of Life.

Family trees represent our genetic history. Tree's rooted to this earth long ago and surpassed all forms of life from the dinosaurs to man.

When you plant a tree, you are giving to future generations, oxygen to breath. Native American Indian's use tree metaphors, in their many legends, to teach their young to understand the circle of life and the relationships of man to the Earth, man to man, man to the Universe.

Next time you pass a tree, take a look at all of the gifts it has given to you- sometimes even without you knowing.

ASPEN - Gifts are that of determination, overcoming your fears and doubts, and a transformation of the self.

BEECH - Gifts are that of tolerance, past knowledge and a softening of criticism to the self and others.

CEDAR - Gifts are that of healing, cleansing and protection from harm to the self and loved ones.

BONSAI - Gifts are that of harmony, peace, balance and all that is good. Many times offered as a gift.

BIRCH - Gifts of new beginnings and cleansing of the past, a renewal of the self, and memories of youth.

APPLE - Gifts are that of magic, youth, beauty, happiness, generosity and immortality as the story of Johnny Appleseed.

ASH - Gifts are that of sacrifice, sensitivity and higher awareness to the self, helps form connection, teaches wisdom, and allows you to surrender to beauty of life.

PINE - Gifts are that of creativity, longevity of life and immortality of awareness.

OAK - Gifts are that of strength, courage, and the mightiest of trees, nobility, endurance and stability. Christians believe it represents Christ.

ORANGE - Gift is that of purity, chastity and generosity to the self and others.

LEMON - Gift is that of fidelity in love.

PALM - Gift is that of peace, opportunity, historical victory and fertility.

MYRTLE - Gift is that of ancient love.

WILLOW - Gift is that of magic, healing, inner vision and dreams. Also associated with death, mourning and to reflect on one's life.

HOLLY - Gift is that of protection, overcoming anger and spiritual warrior's quest. Also used as Christmas decoration.

MAPLE - Gift is that of balance, promise and practicality.

FIR - Gift is that of springtime, patience, and is primary tree used for the Christmas tree tradition started in 1500 in Germany to celebrate faith in eternal life.

CYPRESS - Gift is that of understanding the role of sacrifice, and also associated with death or peaceful rest.

ELDER - Gift is that of birth, death, and associated with the fairy realm in legends.

ELM - Gift is that of strength of will, intuition, faithfulness and endurance.

CHERRY - Gift is that of sweetness of one's character, rebirth, and honesty.

# The Curse

Give to a Bishop that seeks blissful love.
Blessed will be given gifts from above.

Unconditional mirror of truth banished will be.
Days of silence will bare to the tree.

Death will be placed in the givers hand.
Figment of darkness will colden the land.

Set free the guilt of the darkness within.
Bare in mind, the CURSE has no sin.

Recite three times, not by the language of love.
Unity and light will release the dove.

"Tu me Maques"

**Acknowledgements**

I've had so many people cheer me on, I wanted to put them all on this page. I received so much encouragement from many, unfortunately I have but a page. Thank you to anyone I may have missed!

Rhonda Bracewell
Nancy Quatrano (On-target Words)
Michael Ray King (Michael Ray King Publishing)
Shonda Cauley
Chris Balsam
James DuPont
Linda DuPont
Dominic Oliva
Nicholas Oliva
Zachary Oliva
Janelle Barbour
Photo by Jan
Howard Barbour
Phat Puppy Art
Robin Allier
Elizabeth Haddon
Gabe Smith
Angel Eakin
Lisa Stratford
Bill Cooper
Go write Classmates
First Coast Creativity Group
The Beer House Gang
Countrytime Pub gang
Lee and Lesley DuPont Family
Tressie Paytas
Tedder Family
Tudisco Family
Rose Oliva
Chasing Butterflies Series Fans

## About the Author

Jorja DuPont Oliva, author of the Chasing Butterflies Series, is a small business owner, a wife and a mother. Nature and outdoors always have been a love for her. Writing and learning are the pleasures she seeks. She has always been intrigued with things not known and secrets of the past. Jorja is now at work on book three of the Chasing Butterflies Series. Chasing Butterflies in the Unseen Universe 2015/2016. Check out her blog- jorjao2013.com

lizzyanddeemagicalworld.org
Chasing Butterflies
FAN Club
P.O. BOX1774
Bunnell, Florida 32110
EMAIL- jorjao@msn.com